Northanger Abbey – A Critical Essay

Edited by J. McLaine

Olympus Grove Press

Tinfish Type - Librarie du Liban 2015 - Marlinspike 37824

Northanger Abbey – A Critical Study Guide

Contents

Northanger Abbey – A Critical Study Guide has been written with I/GCSE, A Level and IB students in mind. The guide focuses on the novel's relationship to the gothic genre, refers to the historical and literary context and examines elements within the novel such as themes, setting, form and structure. It also contains significant extracts from Austen's novel to do with the gothic as well as several key scenes from Ann Radcliffe's *The Mysteries of Udolpho*.

Narrative, Themes and Setting

Title and Names – *Northanger Abbey* is an apt title for a gothic novel (although one given to the novel by Jane Austen's brother). The thought of the ruins of an ancient abbey would certainly have enticed the contemporary reader and Catherine Morland's response conveys her excitement, albeit in free indirect speech: 'Northanger Abbey! These were thrilling words, and wound up Catherine's feelings to the highest point of ecstasy.' In England such ruins had long inspired a morbid and introspective writing and the contrast between Bath's neo-classical architecture and the anticipation surrounding the gothic style cannot be overstated. Moreover, the name of the ecclesiastical building incorporates the north – where, even after her gothic fantasies are all proven to be groundless, Catherine still entertains the belief that in 'the northern and western extremities' there are places as 'fruitful in horrors' (in keeping with the settings described in Radcliffe's novels). In addition, the word anger conveys a dark emotion frequently found within the gothic. Furthermore, the disyllabic surname Morland equally suggests a suitably gothic setting, and one thoroughly exploited in Emily Bronte's *Wuthering Heights* (1847).

Summary – Austen began *Northanger Abbey* in 1797, although it was not published until after her death; appearing in two volumes in 1818 (the same year *Frankenstein* was first published). *Northanger Abbey* parodies the late eighteenth century gothic with its fainting heroines, hints of horror and the macabre and haunted medieval buildings. The satire's main target is Ann Radcliffe's *The Mysteries of Udolpho* (1794) and Austen has her characters reading and imitating it. *Northanger Abbey* itself concerns a typical Austen heroine, the young Catherine Morland who is taken to the fashionable resort of Bath with her friends the Allens. From there she travels to the eponymous abbey in Gloucestershire, the seat of the Tilneys. As an impressionable girl, Catherine becomes obsessed with the possibility of atrocities having been committed at

Northanger Abbey. Henry proves that Catherine's suspicions concerning the General have no substance, but while she is recovering from her humiliation she finds herself ordered out of the house; the General mistakenly believing her to be penniless. Eleanor's marriage to 'a man of fortune and consequence' and after being restored to a sensible humour by a true understanding of Catherine's worth, the General finally gives his blessing to Henry and Catherine's wedding.

Central to the novel is Catherine's love for Henry Tilney (a clergyman), though to counterbalance the pair Austen puts James Morland under the spell of the unpleasant, scheming Isabella Thorpe. The novel's central theme, common to *Emma* and *Sense and Sensibility* is the peril of confusing life and art: in this instance literature.

Narrator - The use of the first person pronoun appears in the novel but it is largely third person omniscient with the use of free indirect discourse.

Point of View - The narrative voice varies greatly. Sometimes the narrator is content to simply describe events normally; sometimes the narrator addresses the reader directly; and sometimes (especially in the second half of the novel) Austen uses the technique of free indirect discourse (see glossary), in which she describes people and events from a third-person perspective, but in the way that a particular character (in this case, Catherine) sees and understands them.

Tone - Light, ironic, satirical; fond, indulgent or gently mocking when talking about Catherine.

Tense - Immediate past.

Setting - Time: January–April 1798 and then summer, 1798 and autumn and winter 1798/99. Place: the first half of the novel takes place primarily in Bath. The second half takes place thirty miles away from Bath in Northanger Abbey, a large ecclesiastical building that has been converted into the

Tilney's home. Catherine's reaction to the eponymous name is significant, conveying how charged the title would have been to a contemporary reader: 'Northanger Abbey! These were thrilling words, and wound up Catherine's feelings to the highest point of ecstasy.' Later, with 'Henry at her heart, and Northanger Abbey on her lips', Catherine catalogues 'her passion for ancient edifices' with 'long, damp passages' and 'narrow cells' and yearns for 'traditional legends' such as 'some awful memorials of an injured and ill-fated nun.' When the setting shifts to the Abbey, the gothic novel governs Austen's use of description, yet against the reader's expectations she stresses its modernity.

Protagonist - Catherine Morland is seventeen when she stays at the abbey, and the daughter of a clergyman.

Antagonist - Arguably Isabella Thorpe, her brother John Thorpe, or the rather shadowy General Tilney.

Youth - *Northanger Abbey* is concerned with young people and their feelings. Heroines in other Austen novels are a little older than Catherine, and are not as naïve. *Northanger Abbey* portrays Catherine in situations common to teenagers: she faces peer pressure when James, Isabella and John urge her to join them on their carriage trips. Austen plays the youthful Catherine against the older, more experienced Henry Tilney. There are several instances in which the adults comment on the young people, either chuckling at their behaviour or criticizing it. Many readers can sympathize with Catherine once she returns home and immediately becomes sullen and obstinate with her parents.

Reading - There are two kinds of reading in *Northanger Abbey*: reading books or letters and reading people. Catherine Morland is young and inexperienced and she has a hard time distinguishing between the two types of reading. Before Catherine can really enter the world of adulthood, she needs to improve her ability to read people as well as novels. Throughout *Northanger Abbey*, Catherine finds herself unable to 'read between the lines.' She does not notice the obvious romance developing between James and Isabella, she does not understand why Frederick Tilney gets involved, she has no idea why the General is so kind to her. All of these behaviours and motivations are clear to the sensitive reader and to the characters surrounding Catherine. When Catherine finally tries to do some of her own analysis, she gets her perceptions mixed up with those encouraged by her novel reading; she recognizes General Tilney's irritability and the tyrannical control he tries to exert over his children, but she attributes his attitude to the murder of his wife, since such a plot twist occurs frequently in gothic novels.One defining moment for Catherine comes as a result of reading a text. She receives a letter from Isabella, and its contents open Catherine's eyes to Isabella's manipulative, ambitious ways. It would be wrong to say that Catherine is an expert at reading people by the end of the novel, but she does become better at it, and she has learned when imagination can aid perception, and when it can hurt it.

It is also worth mentioning that letters often appear within gothic novels, such as *Udolpho* and *Dracula* (indeed, *Frankenstein* is an epistolary novel, meaning it is made up entirely of letters).

Wealth and Class - In Austen's novels characters are often partly defined by their wealth and status. In *Northanger Abbey*, several characters are preoccupied with material longings. Isabella wants to marry someone rich, and forsakes James in favour of the richer Frederick. Mrs. Allen is obsessed with clothing and shopping, and when talking to Mrs Thorpe, she feels less bad about her own childlessness when she notices the shabbiness of Mrs Thorpe's clothes. The General wants his children to marry into rich and wealthy families, and his personal obsession is with remodelling and landscaping. While giving a guided tour of Northanger Abbey, the General constantly asks Catherine to compare his home and gardens to those of Mr Allen, and is always pleased to find that his belongings are larger or more impressive. In her later novels, Austen linked character's personalities with the particular items they loved. In this early novel, she makes wealth itself the goal and passion of characters like Isabella and General Tilney and both can be seen as greedy fortune-hunters, indeed the latter has a touch of melodrama about him and is perceived by Catherine as having the 'air and attitude of a Montoni' (Montoni being the haughty and misogynistic villain in Radcliffe's *The Mysteries of Udolpho*).

Symbols - Austen draws her portrait of Bath society from her own experience. Northanger Abbey, however, is probably as much a product of the gothic novels that Austen read as it is a product of her own experience. A crumbling ruin is often found in gothic works, some of which feature an abbey, or abandoned and later purchased by some lord or baron who is generally a villain. The holy nature of the abbey becomes ironic in these gothic novels, since terrible things go on there once the lord or baron takes possession.

For Catherine, Northanger Abbey symbolizes an imagined ideal. As soon as she enters the abbey, she begins to think of herself as the heroine of a Gothic novel. Unlike Bath, which is simply a pleasant tourist town, the Abbey is a place of mystery and perhaps even adventure, at least in Catherine's mind. When the Abbey turns out to be disappointingly normal, Catherine uses her memory of the abbeys from her novel reading to make it more sinister.

It must also be remembered that the gothic frequently explores the taboo, and an evil act within an ecclesiastical building juxtaposes the sinister or supernatural with the once hallowed setting.

Themes - Gothic novels; youth; innocence; romance; unfaithfulness (Isabella's); truth and illusion; the perils of fantasy (an awareness of what is real and what is not is established through experience, however not all illusions (as with ambitions in Frankenstein) are extinguished. At the end of the novel the influence of Ann Radcliffe's works is shown to have waned but not to have died within Catherine's mind. 'Charming as were all Mrs. Radcliffe's works, and charming even as were the works of all her imitators, it was not in them perhaps that human nature, at least in the Midland counties of England, was to be looked for.'

Romance is also a key theme within the novel and here, as with *Udolpho* (with Emily and Valancourt), what might be called 'obstacle love' surfaces with Catherine and Henry.

There is also a recurring theme within some gothic novels, and that is the fear of the mob or revolution in general. Frankenstein's creature, for instance, has been seen to symbolise the French revolution: noble intentions to begin with, but ending in terror and bloodshed.

In *Northanger Abbey* there is a brief reference to this contemporary fear when Eleanor believes a conversation between Henry and Catherine about a new novel 'with a frontispiece of two tombstones and a lantern' is actually about a recent event. Austen, after highlighting Eleanor's anxiety, allows Henry to reject her confusion (as he will do with Catherine):

> My dear Eleanor, the riot is only in your own brain... my stupid sister has mistaken all your clearest expressions. You talked of expected horrors in London and instead of instantly conceiving, as any rational creature would have done, that such words could relate only to a circulating library, she immediately pictured to herself a mob of three thousand men assembling in St. George's Fields, the Bank attacked, the Tower threatened, the streets of London flowing with blood, a detachment of the Twelfth Light Dragoons (the hopes of the nation) called up from Northampton to quell the insurgents, and the gallant Captain Frederick Tilney, in the moment of charging at the head of his troop, knocked off his horse by a brickbat from an upper window.

What is again being conveyed here is an apparently female susceptibility for dark imaginings and Henry's ability to articulate those feelings better than Eleanor or, later on, Catherine. Some feminist critics find it hard to admire Jane Austen, disliking her submissive and fanciful female characters and her apparent acceptance of a paternal relationship between men and women. However, men are seen as shallow for a 'good-looking girl', with 'a very ignorant mind' cannot fail to attract a 'clever young man.' Whether the ignorant mind is an added attraction is left open to interpretation.

Structure - *Northanger Abbey* appears to contain two stories: one describes Catherine Morland falling in love with Henry Tilney, while the other focuses on Northanger Abbey and the Gothic genre. It is the latter which is explored in the following pages, though it is important to appreciate that the love story is develops throughout the novel.

Foreshadowing - Foreshadowing often exists in the novel as a parody of Gothic conventions. On the ride to the Abbey, Henry tells Catherine a hypothetical story about her upcoming first night at Northanger, complete with mysterious chests, hidden passages, and villainous doings. This foreshadows Catherine's actual night, when she recreates Henry's prophecy with her imagination.

Major conflict - Catherine, enjoying the frisson of fear produced by her own literary imagination, scares herself and displeases the man who loves her.

Climax - General Tilney sends Catherine away from Northanger Abbey

Falling Action - Catherine returns home, in misery, to Fullerton. She sulks around the house until Henry arrives and proposes to her. Several months later, after the General grudgingly gives his consent, the two are married.

The Denouement - The sense of an impending ending is often part of the experience of reading a novel and half way through the last chapter, the narrator references the expectations of her reader as she approaches the end of the novel. Henry Tilney has proposed to the romantic heroine, the 17-year-old Catherine Morland, and has been accepted. Her parents will not give their consent, however, unless General Tilney, gives his. He is utterly opposed to the alliance because the Morlands are not rich enough. And Catherine will certainly not marry without her own parents' approval. However, Austen's narrator reassures the anxious reader with only a few pages remaining:

> The anxiety, which in this state of their attachment must be the portion of Henry and Catherine, and of all who loved either, as to its final event, can hardly extend, I fear, to the bosom of my readers, who will see in the tell-tale compression of the pages before them, that we are all hastening together to perfect felicity.

And this being what we can call a mock-gothic romance; it must have a happy ending. General Tilney will relent. As the remaining pages are turned, the marriage is approaching and 'We are all hastening together to perfect felicity'. Austen's wry reference to the necessary direction of her narrative thus alerts us to an important fact about the way that a novel ends. An ending is satisfying if it confirms a contract with the reader and thereby fulfils his or her expectations. An ending, leading to a satisfying denouement, is where that contract becomes clear.

The Chronological Structure - Approximate Dates for Catherine's Journal

Christmas, 1797, James Morland with John Thorpe on holiday near London.

1798 Sun-Mon [Jan 21st-22nd]: Catherine's last two days in Wiltshire.

Wed-Thurs [Jan 24th-25th]: Overnight trip to Bath; Catherine and the Allens stay at an inn.

Fri-Sun [Jan 26th-28th]: Three or four days spent in learning new fashions.

Mon [Jan 29th]: Her first ball in Upper Rooms; 'I was there last Monday.'

Tues [Jan 30th]: Catherine goes to theatre; 'I was at the play on Tuesday.'

Wed [Jan 31st]: Catherine goes to concert; 'To the concert?' 'Yes, sir, on Wednesday.'

Fri [Feb 2nd]: Appearance in Lower Rooms, Catherine meets Henry Tilney; 'Friday, went to the Lower Rooms;' she has been there 'about a week;' he had been there 'but for a couple of days' to get lodgings for father and sister.

Sat [Feb 3rd]: Catherine goes to Pump Room, Mr Tilney does not appear; it was this morning he quit Bath for a week; she & Mrs Allen meet Mrs Thorpe & Isabella; that evening they will meet at theatre.

Sun [Feb 4th]: The next day when Catherine and Isabella will meet at chapel.

Sun [Feb 11th]: Isabella, the day before claims to have seen a young man looking adoringly at Catherine.

Mon [Feb 12th]: Eight or nine days after the morning talk and walk after chapel; the two sit, discuss horrid books, and set out in pursuit of two young men; 1:30 pm they meet James Morland and John Thorpe come from Tetbury which they left at 10; two couples to meet in Octagon Room that evening; where Catherine left pining by Thorpe, takes Isabella 3 minutes to desert, humiliated for 10, but then meets Henry Tilney once again, with sister this time, but her dance is pre-taken; he asks another (Miss Smith) and she loses him for the evening; Isabella's utter indifference & hypocrisy.

Tues [Feb 13th]: After a good night's sleep Catherine means to set off for pump-room at one. At half past one the Thorpes drive up with Morland on a 'mild fine day of February'; they return after three; at the Crescent Mrs Allen sees Henry & Eleanor Tilney.

Wed [Feb 14th]: Catherine and Mrs Allen go to pump room; Catherine at last sits with Miss Tilney who came with Mrs Hughes; Henry has gone riding with his father; 'she lay awake ten minutes on Wednesday night'.

Thurs [Feb 15th]: 'She entered the rooms on Thursday evening.' Tilney asks her to dance, Thorpe interrupts with 'I firmly believe you were engaged to me ever since Monday.' Catherine has a conversation with Tilney; Eleanor's invitation to go for a country walk tomorrow; she has known Isabella Thorpe a fortnight.

Fri [Feb 16th]: The 'morrow' brings 'sober morning;' eleven o'clock brings specks of rain (wonderful sequencing of time). It's half past twelve when rains stops; she gets into the carriage by one o'clock; a few minutes after she departs the Tilneys call, but leave no card; evening at Thorpe's; Isabella keeps repeating how glad she is not to be at the ball in Lower Rooms.

Sat [Feb 17th]: Catherine tries to visit Miss Tilney to explain; she is snubbed at door; in the evening she goes to the theatre, but sees no Tilney; he appears in a box at fifth act, she longs for forgiveness and he does come round to their box, so both are not too proud; while she talks with Tilney, he talks to General; it was then that General was led to believe Catherine was an heiress.

Sun [Feb 18th]: 'Monday, Tuesday, Wednesday, Thursday Friday, and Saturday have now passed... the pangs of Sunday only now remain;' scene where Catherine is put under intense pressure by Thorpes and her brother to forego her appointment with Miss Tilney, to lie to her and arrange to have walk on Tuesday rather than following morning (therefore a Monday); Thorpe then says he might go out of town on 'Tuesday;' word Tuesday repeated as they quarrel over it; she refuses to be bullied and goes to the Tilneys' house to tell them the truth.

Mon [Feb 19th]: Catherine and the Tilneys take their walk; later in the morning Catherine to Bond Street. Isabella, John, & James set off at eight for Clifton.

Tues [Feb 20th]: Note from Isabella, Catherine goes to Edgar's Buildings and learns that her brother James and Isabella are engaged; James comes to set out to Wiltshire, and a letter should return tomorrow if he can send it tonight to Salisbury.

Wed [Feb 21st]: Catherine again visits her friend, letter from James arrives; good news.

Thurs [Feb 22nd]: Catherine's talk with Isabel the next day (must be since it was 'yesterday' the Tilneys told her Captain Tilney expected any time). On this night there is the ball in Upper or New Rooms; Tilneys are to be there, Isabella 'consents' to go; Captain Tilney shows and Isabella dances with him.

Sat-Thurs [Feb 24th-Mar1st]: Isabella and Catherine's dialogue over James's letter at last giving details of what parents can do; handsome in offering a living, though two and a half years to wait; on a slightly later day James arrives and received with kindness.

Mon [Mar 5th]: 'Allens had now entered on the sixth week of their stay in Bath;' lodgings have been taken for another fortnight (until Fri, Mar 16th, for Catherine now has 'another three weeks'); however, general will quit Bath 'at the end of another week'.

Tues [Mar 6th] Catherine receives permission by return of post.

Fri [Mar 9th]: Two or three days later Isabella attempts to persuade Catherine to say she has accepted John Thorpe as a suitor. Catherine, sitting next to Tilney and Isabella, overhears the couple (much in the manner that Fanny overhears Henry Crawford and Maria in *Mansfield Park*).

Mon-Tues [Mar 12th-13th]: 'A very few days passed away' during which Catherine observes an altered Isabella.

Wed [Mar 14th]: Catherine learns Captain Tilney is not going away, so she speaks to Henry. Henry comments on their 'week's acquaintance' which tells the reader Isabella began to encourage Tilney only after she had news of the money.

Thurs [Mar 15th]: Last evening of Catherine's stay. Isabella very emotional towards Catherine: looking to curry favour with a supposed sister-in-law.

Here the part of the novel which takes place in Bath ends. What is interesting in the second volume is how time becomes indeterminate just before and after the section's crisis when General Tilney expels Catherine from Northanger. As one might expect from Austen's novels, at her close she suddenly pulls the curtain down and gives only vague indications for the 'happy ending' the reader has been waiting for.

Fri [Mar 16th]: Mr Allen takes Catherine to breakfast at Milsom; the Allens leave at the end of week (now the 16th); Catherine is made uncomfortable by the General; Captain Tilney comes down to breakfast late. They are to leave by ten, three ladies in chaise, father and son in curricle; two hour wait at inn Petty France. Catherine accompanies Henry on the last part of the journey and he entertains her with a gothic description. It is a stormy night and Catherine finds papers in the chest just as the light is extinguished. She tosses and turns until three in the morning.

Sat [Mar 17th]: Wakes up at eight and discovers that the papers are merely laundry bills; Henry to go to Woodston for two or three days; General, Eleanor & Catherine take his customary walk 'in the leafless month of March' Abbey & grounds still beautiful; a walk, girls go in, hour and quarter go by before he returns; by evening Catherine convinced General either murdered his wife or keeps her a prisoner behind a secret door down a staircase in a dungeon (on Monday Catherine says Eleanor took her over the greatest part of the house on 'Saturday').

Sun [Mar 18th]: 'It was Sunday', two services, sees the memorial to Mrs Tilney, sky fades between six and seven. Note the close use of the setting sun: 'It was Sunday, and the whole time between morning and afternoon service was required by the general in exercise abroad or eating cold meat at home; and great as was Catherine's curiosity, her courage was not equal to a wish of exploring them after dinner, either by the fading light of the sky between six and seven o'clock, or by the yet more partial though stronger illumination of a treacherous lamp'.

Mon [Mar 19th]: The ladies view Mrs Tilney's portrait; the General interrupts them as they are about to enter Mrs Tilney's chamber; Catherine goes to her room; Eleanor says her father wanted her only to answer a note. At four o'clock Catherine visits Mrs Tilney's room by herself and is disappointed to find a bright bedroom. She is confronted by Henry Tilney, the latter having returned unexpectedly from his parsonage.

Tues [Mar 20th]: Catherine feels humiliated by her misjudgements, yet the 'lenient hand of time did much for her by insensible gradations in the course of another day'.

Wed-Thurs [Mar 21st-29th]: 'For nine successive mornings, Catherine wondered... on the tenth, when she entered the breakfast-room, her first object was a letter...'

Fri [Mar 30th]: The letter from James announcing the end of his engagement; he left Bath 'yesterday,' so perhaps the Wednesday 25. Indeterminate time passing ending on following Saturday: includes 'frequent canvassing' of subject of Isabella Thorpe and Captain Tilney. Henry and Eleanor refuse to believe that Captain Tilney will marry a girl with no money or position.

Sat [Apr 7]: Henry leaves 'two days before I intended it'. Captain Tilney drops Isabella to pursue Charlotte Davis.

Wed [Apr 11]: On 'Wednesday, I think, Henry, you may expect us... about a quarter before one on Wednesday'. By ten o'clock, the chaise and four conveyed the two from the abbey; and, after an agreeable drive of almost twenty miles, they entered Woodston. At four they were to dine, and at six to set off on their return. Isabella writes to Catherine.

Thurs [Apr 12]: Isabella's April letter arrives. Isabella is to leave Bath. Captain Tilney left two days ago and for two days before that had dropped her.

Indeterminate time: Soon after receiving Isabella's letter the General goes to London for a week; Catherine in fourth week of her stay, turning into fifth. Eleanor is distressed at the notion Catherine's departure so visit continues. John Thorpe tells an exaggerated story of Catherine's poverty, as he had her wealth.

Sat [Apr 21]: Henry is obliged 'to leave them on Saturday for a couple of nights'. At 'eleven o'clock' Catherine and Eleanor are still up when the General returns unexpectedly. Eleanor later tells Catherine that she must leave Northanger.

Sun [Apr 22-Apr 23]: Transparent excuse for kicking Catherine out is General's 'engagement' to go 'on Monday' to Lord Longtown's in Hereford 'for a fortnight'; Henry returns to Abbey ('two days before' he turns up at Fullerton. After a quarrel with his father leaves 'almost instantly;' returns to the parsonage where 'many solitary hours were required to compose'. On this day Catherine wakes up pale and not in spirits; writes to Eleanor. Catherine and her mother walk a quarter of a mile to visit Mrs Allen; not quite or just three months; Mrs Allen remembers first time they were in Lower Rooms (Fri, Feb 2nd) because of silk gloves, where Catherine met Henry.

Tues [Apr 24]: Henry sets out for Fullerton 'on the afternoon of the following day'.

Wed [Apr 25]: After 'two days' and third night of restless sad behaviour Catherine's mother scolds her; goes out to seek edifying book, detained by 'family matters' as well, so gone for 15 minutes, during which time Henry Tilney shows up; he manages to take Catherine on a walk alone to the Allens wherein he explains and proposes; applies to her family for her hand in marriage.

Summer, 1798: Eleanor Tilney marries a man of 'fortune and consequence,' an 'unexpected accession of fortune and titles,' the man who left the washing bill.

Late autumn, 1798 or early winter, 1799: Catherine Morland and Henry Tilney marry 'within a twelvemonth from the first day of their meeting,' aged 18 and 26.

An Introduction to *The Mysteries of Udopho*

Radcliffe utilized traditional gothic elements such as the backdrop of an old castle situated in a wild and remote landscape, and included an endangered heroine (Emily), her lover (Valancourt), and a tyrannical older man (Montoni). The sublime landscape, the mountain ranges, raging torrents and immense forests which Emily encounters while travelling to the Castle of Udolpho is used to create suspense and atmosphere. Valancourt is confined within a labyrinthine castle, thus incorporating typically Gothic themes such as isolation and, with Emily, the fear of being trapped. Emily is an orphaned and persecuted maiden prone to fainting when overwhelmed by emotion, and, of course, there is physical and psychological terror.

With *The Mysteries of Udolpho* it is worth observing that the narrative voice clearly conveys Emily's feelings on her way to Montoni's castle. After seeing the Apennines 'in their darkest horror' the reader is once more encouraged to identify with the protagonist:

> 'Emily gazed with melancholy awe upon the castle, which she understood to be Montoni's; for, though it was now lighted up by the setting sun, the gothic greatness of its features, and its mouldering walls of dark grey stone, rendered it a gloomy and sublime object. As she gazed, the light died away on its walls, leaving a melancholy purple tint, which spread deeper and deeper, as the thin vapour crept up the mountain, while the battlements above were still tipped with splendour. From those, too, the rays soon faded, and the whole edifice was invested with the solemn duskiness of evening. Silent, lonely, and sublime, it seemed to stand the sovereign of the scene, and to frown defiance on all, who dared to invade its solitary reign. As the twilight deepened, its features became more awful in obscurity, and

Emily continued to gaze, till its clustering towers were alone seen, rising over the tops of the woods, beneath whose thick shade the carriages soon after began to ascend. The extent and darkness of these tall woods awakened terrific images in her mind, and she almost expected to see banditti start up from under the trees.'

Montoni, like many gothic or Radcliffean villains, is both articulate and intelligent. He is the darkly irresistible villain and with his 'air of conscious superiority', he hypnotises others into compliance. A precursor to Byronic anti-heroes, he broods as much as he acts. The following exchange gives an indication of his attitude towards women, as well as the narrator's own stance towards her heroine:

'I fear, sir, it was a more than common interest, that detained me,' said Emily calmly; 'for of late I have been inclined to think, that of compassion is an uncommon one. But how could I, could YOU, sir, witness Count Morano's deplorable condition, and not wish to relieve it?'
'You add hypocrisy to caprice,' said Montoni, frowning, 'and an attempt at satire, to both; but, before you undertake to regulate the morals of other persons, you should learn and practise the virtues, which are indispensable to a woman--sincerity, uniformity of conduct and obedience.'

Emily, who had always endeavoured to regulate her conduct by the nicest laws, and whose mind was finely sensible, not only of what is just in morals, but of whatever is beautiful in the female character, was shocked by these words; yet, in the next moment, her heart swelled with the consciousness of having deserved praise, instead of censure, and she was proudly silent.

After Emily is made a 'prisoner of the castle' the reader is given a typical description:

>'The night was stormy; the battlements of the castle appeared to rock in the wind, and, at intervals, long groans seemed to pass on the air, such as those, which often deceive the melancholy mind, in tempests, and amidst scenes of desolation.'

The moral is given in the penultimate paragraph:

>'O! useful may it be to have shown, that, though the vicious can sometimes pour affliction upon the good, their power is transient and their punishment certain; and that innocence, though oppressed by injustice, shall, supported by patience, finally triumph over misfortune!'

Northanger Abbey and the Gothic

Gothic novels – According to Horace Walpole, the author of *The Castle of Otranto* (1764) modern fiction had been too preoccupied with the commonplace, everyday life. In following the laudable aim of giving an authentic picture of the life and the manners of the time, novelists had neglected the strong life of the imagination. In striving for verisimilitude (a feature of which is the letter writing in *Frankenstein*, an epistolary novel written when the form had become unfashionable) authors, according to Walpole, had failed to explore the fantastical, the lawless and violent. What is also interesting to note about *The Castle of Otranto* is its subtitle: *A Gothic Story.* This is arguably the first application of the word 'Gothic' to a literary work and he is credited to have invented the new genre. When his novel was published, the subtitle meant something like 'a barbarous tale' - and so it was, with ghosts, tunnels and a sexually enraged medieval prince.

Between 1764 and 1818, when *Northanger Abbey* was published, the gothic genre had flourished almost unchecked. However, Jane Austen's gothic parody skilfully satirizes the form and conventions of the genre. In particular, Austen targeted Ann Radcliffe, the author of gothic novels such as *A Sicilian Romance* (1790), *The Romance of the Forest* (1791), and *The Mysteries of Udolpho* (1794). Catherine reads *Udolpho* during her time at Bath, and it is implied that she has read similar novels before, and Isabella has a library of other gothic novels that the women plan to read once Catherine has finished *Udolpho*.

Gothic novels and their conventions occur throughout the novel. On the ride from Bath to Northanger Abbey, Henry invents a humorous mock-prophetic story about Catherine's first night in the Abbey, making subtle references to several different gothic novels, most of which were well-known at the time.

Aside from Henry's parody of gothic novels on the way to *Northanger Abbey*, two other sequences poke fun at the genre. In one, Catherine unlocks the mysterious cabinet, expecting it to contain something horrible, and finds only laundry bills. In another, Catherine imagines that the General is a wife-murderer and goes to investigate the late Mrs. Tilney's bedroom. When Henry catches her at this task and scolds her, it is not amusing, as is Catherine's discovery of the laundry bills. We feel sympathy for Catherine, who is terribly embarrassed in front of Henry. In the scenes leading up to the confrontation with Henry, it is almost disturbing to read of Catherine's paranoid assumptions that everything the General does stems from a guilty conscience. Catherine becomes almost unhinged by her own imagination. Although the actual crime turns out to be nonexistent, Austen captures some of the psychological tension typical of gothic novels by chronicling Catherine's delusions. So although she parodies the gothic genre, Austen also makes use of some of its techniques.

In *The Mysteries of Udolpho* (1794) an incident occurs which is repeated Northanger Abbey. In Mrs Radcliffe's novel Emily St Aubert, the heroine imprisoned within the castle of Udolpho, does what every Gothic heroine appears to do:

> Emily, bending over the body, gazed, for a moment, with an eager, frenzied eye; but in the next, the lamp dropped from her hand …

Northanger Abbey replicates the lamp-dropping incident not once but twice. Not only with Henry Tilney's parody on the way to Northanger, but also when Catherine discovers what she, with her macabre imagination fed on a diet of gothic horror, believes to be a 'precious manuscript' Here the omniscient narrator relates how 'A lamp could not have expired with more awful effect'. Yet Jane Austen's heroine, like Mrs Radcliffe's with her 'eager … eye' when the body is discovered, feels that the manuscript has been so 'wonderfully found' and it is greeted as 'wonderfully accomplishing the morning's prediction. The morning's prediction of course relates to Henry Tilney's parody.

However, it must be remembered that *Udolpho* contains extreme situations and unlikely characters, setting it apart from the domestic realism found in *Northanger Abbey*. What Austen relies upon is the reader having a lot of background information, an understanding of the protagonist and the genre. The young woman Austen is writing about is therefore a fair reflection of her contemporary reading public.

Revision Tasks

Complete diary entries for Catherine's journal covering the following dates:

1798
Fri Jan 26th First day in Bath: spent in learning new fashions.

Mon Jan 29th Her first Ball in Upper Rooms; 'I was there last Monday.'
Fri Feb 2nd Appearance in Lower Rooms, Catherine meets Henry Tilney; 'Friday, went to the Lower Rooms;' she has been there 'about a week;' he had been there 'but for a couple of days' to get lodgings for father and sister.

Sat Feb 3rd Catherine goes to Pump Room, Mr Tilney does not appear; it was this morning he quit Bath for a week; she & Mrs Allen meet Mrs Thorpe & Isabella; that evening they will meet at theatre.

Essay Titles with Guidance on How to Answer

Catherine is inexperienced and innocent at the beginning of the novel. How has she changed by the end of the novel?

Northanger Abbey is a bildungsroman, a coming-of-age tale in which the heroine sheds her naiveté. In the beginning, Catherine does not see the obvious flirtation between her brother James and her friend Isabella, and she does not understand what Isabella is doing by flirting with Captain Tilney. Catherine has difficulty identifying people's motivations, which, as Henry points out, causes her to assume that people do things for the same unimpeachable reasons she would. As a result, Catherine thinks well of almost everyone, and is frequently too charitable to such people as Isabella and John Thorpe. As the novel progresses, Catherine starts trying to understand people and their motivations, although this pursuit is influenced by her overactive imagination. She attributes General Tilney's grumpiness and odd behaviour to guilt over murdering his new wife. After Henry scolds her for this terrible and unfounded suspicion, Catherine comes to a new realization about the nature of people. She understands that people can be both good and bad, because real life is never as black-and-white as it is in the novels she reads.

What makes Catherine think the General murdered his wife? Why does she realize her mistake so quickly?

There are several reasons why Catherine starts to believe that the General killed his wife. The first is that she has just read a gothic novel, *The Mysteries of Udolpho*, by Ann Radcliffe, and has come to associate old buildings like Northanger Abbey with the mysterious buildings she encounters in her reading. Catherine arrives at the Abbey feeling that she is in a gothic novel herself. As she later admits to herself, she arrives at the Abbey 'craving to be scared,' and when she finds it to be a very boring place, she makes up her own secrets. When Catherine finds out that Mrs. Tilney died of a mysterious illness nine years earlier, and that Eleanor was not there at the time of her mother's death, she feels her suspicions of General Tilney are confirmed. After that, every odd quirk of the General's makes Catherine feel certain that he has a guilty conscience. Her desire to be scared becomes a self-fulfilling prophecy. Soon, Catherine is swept up in a paranoid fantasy, and even entertains the idea that Mrs Tilney is alive and held captive in a dungeon beneath the Abbey. She does not wonder why the General would murder his wife. She sees him as a one-dimensional villain from a novel, a purely evil person who would certainly murder his wife without a second thought. Once Henry chastises her for her morbid imaginings, and shows her how illogical her suspicions were, Catherine wakes up from her fantasy and realizes how silly it was. She begins to understand that the General may be gruff and sometimes mean to his children, but he is not evil, and he is not a murderer.

Is General Tilney the antagonist in the novel? Why or why not?

The antagonist of the novel is the character who opposes the protagonist's goals. For most of the novel, General Tilney does his best to make Catherine feel comfortable, because he thinks she is rich and wants her to marry his son, Henry. So to Catherine, the protagonist, he is very pleasant. To his children, the General is alarmingly bossy. He has a generally gruff nature that makes him seem unpleasant. But he does his utmost to make Catherine feel welcome until the end of her stay, when he acts badly by sending her away abruptly, with no explanation. This is the most cruel thing that anyone does to Catherine in the course of the novel. We discover later that the General sent Catherine away because John Thorpe told him that her family had no money. This infuriated the General, who had hoped to marry John into a rich family. Complicating the matter is the fact that Catherine has imagined the General as a villain from a Gothic horror novel. Since the reader sees the General through Catherine's eyes, the General seems to become a true villain, at least for a few chapters. Even after Catherine realizes her mistake, a lingering doubt about the General and his behaviour remains, especially when he sends Catherine home so rudely. Although the General behaves badly, however, he is not indisputably villainous. On one hand, he is greedy, rude to his children, and obsessed with wealth and class. On the other, he is a caring father and capable of being a gracious host to Catherine. An arrogant man like John Thorpe, were he to play a larger part in the novel, could easily become the antagonist. However, no one in the novel actively, constantly works to thwart Catherine or her hopes, which means the novel has no true antagonist.

Consider some of the ways in which Jane Austen uses gothic settings in Northanger Abbey.

This question focuses on Jane Austen's use of gothic settings and any response should include Northanger Abbey itself and point out the significance of the name of the house to admirers of gothic fiction. You would also be expected to talk about the images it conjures up in Catherine's mind when she hears the name. There should also be discussion of how the reality does not live up to Catherine's gothic imaginings when she first sees it - 'to an imagination which had hoped for the smallest divisions and the heaviest stone-work, for painted glass, dirt and cobwebs, the difference was very distressing.' - as well as Catherine's bedroom at the Abbey. Catherine's exploration of the General's wife's room and the 'forbidden door' could be seen as significant as well as Henry Tilney's crushing response to Catherine's gothic expectations. The effects Jane Austen creates using gothic language and imagery and devices, which build up suspense in connection with setting, should not be neglected and it would be worth, certainly at A Level, considering the way in which gothic settings are used to create humour and for satirical purposes.

Essay Titles

What are the advantages of Austen's use of free indirect discourse? What is the effect of it in scenes like the one in which Catherine opens the mysterious cabinet?

How far does Jane Austen convince us that in the characters of *Northanger Abbey* there is a 'general though unequal mixture of good and bad'?

The marriage of Henry and Catherine happens very quickly at the end of the novel, almost as if it is an afterthought. Does the narrative haste lessen the significance of the wedding? Why do you think the end is so abrupt?

Some say the climax of the novel occurs when General Tilney sends Catherine away. However, some say the climax occurs when Catherine sneaks into the late Mrs. Tilney's room and discovers nothing, and then gets caught and scolded by Henry. Which do you think is the climax and why?

Some critics think *Northanger Abbey* criticizes the people attracted to resorts like Bath. Do you think this is true?

To what extent do you agree that, in *Northanger Abbey*, Jane Austen is simply ridiculing the gothic genre?

How far do you agree with the idea that a preoccupation with the gothic is presented as a female vice?

Consider the view that, throughout the novel, desire is more closely linked to horror than to love.

How significant a part does Henry Tilney's sister, Eleanor, play in the novel?

Gothic writing is thrilling because it allows us to think the unthinkable. How far do you agree with this view?

What extent do you think gothic writing is a troubling exploration of the unknown?

How far do you agree with the view that gothic writing shows that human beings are naturally inclined to be evil rather than good?

Key Quotations

In what is referred to as a 'closed book' exam you will be required to learn quotations in order to illustrate your point or opinion. A quotation can be a single word, a short phrase or a line or two. Examiners will not expect you to quote several lines and to do so, at least without a close critical analysis of each line, is likely to be counterproductive. Below are lines taken from the novel which give you the opportunity to focus on key passages within the text.

Isabella's conversation with Catherine: 'when you have finished *Udolpho*, we will read the Italian together; and I have made out a list of ten or twelve more of the same kind for you.'

'Have you, indeed! How glad I am! What are they all?'

'I will read you their names directly; here they are, in my pocketbook. *Castle of Wolfenbach, Clermont, Mysterious Warnings, Necromancer of the Black Forest, Midnight Bell, Orphan of the Rhine, and Horrid Mysteries*. Those will last us some time.'

'Yes, pretty well; but are they all horrid, are you sure they are all horrid?'

'Yes, quite sure; for a particular friend of mine, a Miss Andrews, a sweet girl, one of the sweetest creatures in the world, has read every one of them.'

In Bath 'Catherine was then left to the luxury of a raised, restless, and frightened imagination over the pages of *Udolpho*.'

'Do not you think *Udolpho* the nicest book in the world?' Here Catherine conveys her love of the gothic and her inappropriate or clumsy use of language. Henry's response is to intentionally misinterpret for humorous effect: 'The nicest by which I suppose you mean the neatest. That must depend upon the binding.' However, Catherine insists on calling it 'a nice book.'

Henry: 'I have read all Mrs. Radcliffe's works, and most of them with great pleasure. The Mysteries of *Udolpho*, when I had once begun it, I could not lay down again; I remember finishing it in two days my hair standing on end the whole time.'

Catherine, having been reassured by Henry's enjoyment of the novel: 'and now I shall never be ashamed of liking *Udolpho*.

Isabella Thorpe: 'My attachments are always excessively strong.'
'Of all the things in the world, inconstancy is my aversion.'
'Amazing', 'Odious' and 'Horrid' convey something of Isabella's speech, and the verbal exaggerations can be seen in Catherine's own speech (Austen showing Isabella's influence).

'Northanger Abbey – these were thrilling words, and wound up Catherine's feelings to... ecstasy!' 'Among the Alps and the Pyrenees, perhaps, there were no mixed characters (meaning either villains or heroes).

Henry and Catherine's conversation just before their arrival at Northanger is a key passage within the novel for anyone studying the gothic and is included towards the end of the novel.

The word 'gothic' appears four times in the novel, three used to describe the windows at Northanger Abbey and once to describe the quadrangle as 'rich in Gothic ornaments'.

On being left in her room at Northanger: 'Her fearful curiosity' is awoken by a large chest, an 'object so well calculated to interest and alarm.' She is disappointed and 'astonished, to find a 'white cotton counterpane.'

Retiring to her room after dinner: 'The night was stormy.... Yes, these were characteristic sounds; they brought to her recollection a countless variety of dreadful situations and horrid scenes, which such buildings had witnessed, and such storms ushered in.' Her discovery of the 'manuscript' is again included at the end of the study guide and is worthy of close analysis.

Catherine at Northanger has 'an imagination resolved on alarm' with a mind before she entered the abbey 'craving to be frightened.' 'She saw that the infatuation had been created, the mischief settled, long before her quitting Bath, and it seemed as if the whole might be traced to the influence of that sort of reading which she had there indulged.'

Henry Tilney: 'Remember the country and the age we live in... does our education prepare us for such atrocities?'

'Charming as were all Mrs. Radcliffe's works, and charming even as were the works of all her imitators, it was not in them perhaps that human nature, at least in the Midland counties of England, was to be looked for.' How Catherine reflects on the gothic after her fantasy has been shattered is also included at the end of the study guide.

Studying the Gothic

Northanger Abbey is a direct parody of the type of gothic novel which was being written at the end of the eighteenth century and when studying a gothic text it is useful to consider certain key cultural and literary oppositions: barbarity versus civilisation; the wild versus the domestic (or domesticated); the supernatural versus the apparently 'natural'; that which lies beyond human understanding compared with that which we ordinarily encompass; the unconscious as opposed to the waking mind; passion versus reason; night versus day. Try applying these oppositions to *Northanger Abbey* and see where they take you in understanding the essential qualities of this genre.

It is also useful to make a distinction between 'terror' and 'horror': 'terror' is to be thought of as something more shadowy, more insubstantial, harder to pin down, as a suggestion or threat which builds over time; 'horror' stands for a gross physical shock, something which the reader can visualise. 'To awaken thrilling horror' was Mary Shelley's aim with *Frankenstein* (an aim, no doubt, which was more easily achieved with her contemporary reader than with today's). It is worth considering how we can define horror and terror today, in comparison to when *Northanger Abbey* written. It is also worth thinking about how they contribute to the central mood of the gothic, which is fear. This mood generally has something to do with the past, with 'what comes back', with the revenant or the so-called undead. Usually the ghost that returns has some connection with an evil deed the protagonist has committed in the past, although occasionally there seems little clear reason for the 'return'. Freud identified the unconscious as that place in the mind from which nothing ever goes away and there is a clear connection with the past, the world of dreams and the unconscious mind. In dreams the dreamer is frequently being chased, hence the pursued maiden. Moreover, guilty thoughts and illicit desires can surface, as with Victor Frankenstein's dream of his dead mother and Elizabeth.

Therefore, as well as considering the cultural oppositions, and how our understanding of horror has changed over the years, it is also worth dwelling upon how the unconscious mind is conveyed to the reader. Austen, within her gothic parody, clearly uses free indirect discourse and this allows the reader a direct insight into the mind of Catherine Morland.

Conventions and Elements of the Gothic

The novel which is thought to have started the gothic tradition is Horace Walpole's *The Castle of Otranto* (1764). It became a popular genre in the late eighteenth century, and its conventions have been used by authors ever since. In the nineteenth century, parodies of the genre started appearing, because its conventions were so widely known. *Northanger Abbey* explores the perils of fantasy with Catherine's outlandish suppositions incorporating gothic motifs and ideas. The conventions commonly found elements within gothic novels are listed below:

Sinister settings – castles, ecclesiastical buildings, ruins, dungeons, secret passages, winding stairs, haunted buildings, dark and gloomy places.
Sublime and/or inhospitable landscapes – rugged mountains, thick forests, generally bad weather.
Omens, ancestral curses and secrets.
Representation and stimulation of fear, horror and the macabre.
Tyrants, villains, maniacs, or simply focusing on the darkness of men's hearts, and other dark and bloody subjects.
Persecuted maidens, femme fatales, madwomen (think of first wives locked away in attics, incestuous sibling relationships, etc.).
Ghosts, monsters, demons, succubus, vampires.
Byronic heroes – intelligent, sophisticated and educated, but struggling with emotional conflicts, a troubled past and 'dark' attributes.
A combination of horror and romance....an appreciation of the joys of extreme emotion, the thrills of fearfulness and awe inherit in the sublime, and a quest for atmosphere.
Use of primitive, medieval, mysterious elements and horrifying, grotesque, supernatural events.
An atmosphere of degeneration and decay.

Early gothic fiction was popular with female readers and thus explores themes relevant to the implied reader: the curious female (versus the solitary male on his quest for knowledge).

The Literary and Historical Context

Since the publication of Walpole's *The Castle of Otranto* gothic literature has engendered a taste for the distasteful and an appetite for the pleasures of the flesh, although to the modern reader Walpole's giant helmets and speaking pictures now seem rather ridiculous. The works which were perceived in the late eighteenth century as most distinctively gothic were those of Ann Radcliffe – chiefly *The Mysteries of Udolpho* and *The Italian* – and *The Monk* by Matthew Lewis. Mary Shelley's *Frankenstein*, though now usually seen as gothic, appeared a little late in the period and was arguably more concerned with the perils of scientific experimentation than with the problems of ghosts and haunting which preoccupied the gothic. The second wave in the late nineteenth century was, perhaps, an accompaniment to *fin de siècle* notions of decadence and degeneration: Bram Stoker's *Dracula*, Robert Louis Stevenson's *The Strange Case of Dr Jekyll and Mr Hyde*, Wells's *The Island of Doctor Moreau* and Oscar Wilde's *The Picture of Dorian Gray*. Later, twentieth-century gothic writing, from H.P. Lovecraft to Robert Bloch, has continued to test the limits of taste and horror and a penchant for the suburban gothic has surfaced, particularly in film. Recently, with novels such as Susan Hill's *The Woman in Black* and Stephen Bywater's *Night of the Damned* we have the historical gothic with settings either incorporating the motif of the haunted house or ranging far and wide with the latter set in the Amazon jungle in the 1930s.

However, to trace the gothic back to its roots we have to consider the original Goths, who have been credited, at least in part, with the downfall of the Roman Empire and the sack of Rome. Sadly the Goths left almost no written records, and were mostly unheard of until the 'first gothic revival' in the late eighteenth century. In Britain this revival involved a series of attempts to 'return to roots', in contrast to the classical model revered in the earlier eighteenth century. (Compare the neo-classical poetry of Alexander Pope to that of Wordsworth and you'll see a switch from the ornate and erudite to the relatively plain use of language and structure.)

The notion of the gothic as a reaction against the neo-classical tradition had a considerable impact during the Romantic period, and influenced almost all the major Romantic writers in different ways. William Blake was an upholder of the gothic as against the classical and Coleridge's ballad *The Rime of the Ancient Mariner* is arguably gothic in its use of supernatural machinery. The earliest writers of the gothic also made it clear that they were 'against reason' – they did not accept the classic Enlightenment view that humans are mainly driven by reason. On the contrary: the gothic reminds us that we are mainly driven by our passions. This may be a good or a bad thing. It may be a good thing insofar as we might feel emotional intensity towards certain people or causes; it may be a bad thing insofar as it drives us into obsession or madness. At all events, the gothic deals in illicit desires, in what is prohibited by society, in emotional extremes, whether terror or love, and terrifying forces.

It is against this background that we see the emergence of *Northanger Abbey* and an architectural revival which looked back to the great English medieval cathedrals for inspiration, rather than to the Greek and Roman architecture which had so greatly influenced the period of the Enlightenment. (The Palace of Westminster, better known as the Houses of Parliament, was rebuilt after a fire in 1839 in the gothic style. In contrast, the White House was completed in 1800 and built in the neo-classical style.) The crucial feature of the gothic style was a medieval other-worldliness with ornate features and soaring perspectives – part of the gothic preoccupation with the sublime.

Therefore the gothic texts can be seen as a reaction against the rational discourse that marked the literature and philosophy of The Age of Reason. Instead of Reason and Rationality the Imagination was set free; typified, some might argue, by Catherine's fantasies and wildly-connected impressions. The boundaries of logic and sense were breached and, instead, the sensational and the sensual were celebrated.

Gothic texts allowed readers to think the unthinkable; to sublimate their innermost desires within the pages of books that were in their very existence an affront to the intellectual establishment. As such they became a way of subverting the establishment. Novels that were concerned with outsiders and whose protagonists flouted the natural order became the obvious vehicle for attacking the safe, central values of a society that smugly turned its back on those who were not born into the comfort of money, education and power. The power and passion of gothic literature seemed eminently suited to the iconoclasts, writers such as Lewis, Godwin, Shelley, who wished to challenge the status quo. Often the repressive regime is represented by an ancient order that resists change and any challenge to its autocratic rule. The heroes are those who seek to overturn this authority and establish the freedom to develop their individuality. In this sense the gothic can echo the early ideals of the Romantic movement which sought to revolutionise society.

From this time on, the gothic has continued to exert an influence. We can find it in the ghost story, which became extraordinarily popular during the Edwardian period when writers such as Arthur Conan Doyle and M.R. James wrote a number of distinctly gothic tales. And we can find it in the more contemporary period with the evolution of the horror story in the hands of writers like those already mentioned and in the work of Angela Carter and Neil Gaiman. We can find it too in parodies of the gothic, which is where Jane Austen's early nineteenth-century satire *Northanger Abbey*, sits within genre.

Language and Setting

The language in gothic novels tends to be passionate, excessive, emotive; sensational and unrestrained by taste or moderation. The construction of the plot and the depiction of character – particularly in the early texts – are often crude and fantastical. There is little that is refined, rational or tasteful in the pages of these self-consciously lurid stories. Gothic texts tend to be about transgression, overstepping boundaries and entering a realm of the unknown. In this realm the ordinary is displaced by the extraordinary, the normal becomes the paranormal and the unconscious is as vivid, vital and valid as the conscious.

In this environment it becomes difficult to orientate one's self: it is often a dark world where winding passages lead deeper and deeper into an uncanny and uncertain world. Forests, wildernesses, extremes of nature predominate. The rational world is left far behind, reason no longer rules. The improbable is entirely possible and the impossible becomes ever more probable. Often the protagonist is presented with a baffling series of choices with no clear sense of what the right one might be.

The *ancien regime* (or old order) is exemplified in old buildings – castles, abbeys, towers and so on. These features have become a sort of gothic shorthand that signifies dominance, barbarity and the dead hand of authority. These buildings are peopled by autocratic fathers, uncles, counts and kings.

Paradoxically, gothic literature also lent itself to those who wished to warn society against the effects of breaking with the natural order: the protagonists who strayed off the path of reason, order or decorum often came face-to-face with the consequences of their actions rendered all the more terrible in the lurid world of the gothic text. Darkly attractive strangers who tempt the innocent and naïve are transformed into demonic villains who are only just defeated by some force of righteousness, a personification of conventional morality, and the weeping victim is led back to safety a wiser and better person. The consequences of transgression are clearly delineated and the boundaries between order and chaos are endorsed and reinforced in the resurrection of an acceptable moral order (see Radcliffe, Carter, Bywater).

Gothic texts are set in foreign locations. At first these locations were literally exotic and far away – Italy, Spain, Arabia, Middle Europe but fairly quickly sublime landscapes closer to home were explored – Yorkshire, Scotland, Ireland, the Lake District. The fact that the 'foreign' could exist in the reader's own neighbourhood made it all the more frightening. In *Northanger Abbey* there is very little description of Bath, but social conventions with the backdrop of a ball, walk or drive are carefully considered. When the setting of the novel shifts to Northanger Abbey the description of the eponymous building is soon at odds with Catherine's expectations. Here, instead of the physical setting, the landscape of the mind becomes the ultimate other world where the self is lost in a welter of barely suppressed urges and desires.

Again the process of reading/viewing the gothic becomes a reflexive metaphor: it describes itself. The viewer/reader is reading an externalised representation of his/her fascination with the unknowable – selfhood itself. Writers such as Austen, Stevenson and Poe anticipate the works of Freud in their exploration of the Unconscious.

Safe in the fictive world of gothic literature the reader/viewer can vicariously experience the trials of those who have transgressed the boundaries of society, morality or sanity. They can overstep the margins of reasonable behaviour secure in the knowledge that they retain the power to shut the book, close the text and return to the rational world.

In each of these texts there is a clearly defined threshold over which the protagonist and the reader must step. It may be represented as a physical boundary – the dividing line between the civilised and the natural world as in *Wuthering Heights*. It might be a social line – the girl breaks free from the constraints of her family's expectations and rushes into the arms of some dubious stranger with an altogether 'other' agenda as in so many of Radcliffe's novels.

It might be a moral line where the protagonist breaks a moral law – perhaps he has the temerity to imitate his Maker and breathe life into the inanimate.

The Female Victim

At the heart of the gothic text is the tension provided by the possible violation of innocence – the concept of 'virtue in distress'. In the first flowering of the gothic as a genre the innocent victim was almost exclusively female. Her chastity was the object of the villain's desire and the novel's landscapes and imagery often provided an obvious objective correlative for this sexual threat. Swords were raised, arrows let loose, doors forced and defences breached. Victims found themselves pursued down tortuous passages with no clear sight of an escape route: they were trapped in impossible situations – and, as the genre developed, these were often of their own making. Sometimes their situation was made worse by the fact that their violation seemed to be legitimised by the laws of the land – the idea of the *droit du seigneur* Angela Carter memorably pastiches the latter in *The Bloody Chamber*.

The preponderance of suffering women frequently foregrounds a struggle between the genders, a struggle in which men always have the upper hand. Texts such as *Jane Eyre*, of course, partially reverse this idea, since Jane, in a sense, 'wins'; but what she wins is an aged and blinded version of the man she loves. Certainly a great deal of Gothic fiction has been written by women, from Radcliffe through to Rice; and, much Gothic fiction, emblematically *Dracula*, seems to form itself around what psychologists might call 'eve-of-wedding fantasies' – those fantasies of lost freedom which women in particular have – or have had – before marriage (though ironically at the height of the Gothic, women had little freedom to lose!). There is a whole strand of criticism devoted to the 'female Gothic' – one of its main arguments hinges on the motif of the castle and its relation to the constrained domestic sphere which most women, in the late eighteenth and early nineteenth centuries, were forced to inhabit.

In *Northanger Abbey* there is a tension between the passive and the active state, the conflict between the temptation of succumbing to temptation, and indulging in a fantasy. Catherine Morland can be seen to enter into what

Carter's female protagonist in *The Bloody Chamber* calls the kingdom of the unimaginable. As a reader, and certainly for the female reader of the early nineteenth century, there is the vicarious thrill when the protagonist encounters the unimaginable and entertains taboo thoughts. In Austen's novel Catherine becomes increasingly active until Henry Tilney confronts her in his mother's bedroom. Seeing oneself as others see us is a quality many writers stress the importance of. It complements both the importance of self-knowledge and the acceptance of change from innocence to experience.

In *Frankenstein*, and putting aside Victor playing God and the question of how human ambition might overstep the boundaries of creation, we also have a gender argument, since the protagonist also usurps the role of women in reproduction. It is also worth considering the novel from a biographical or even psychoanalytical perspective, informed by the fact that Mary Shelley's own mother died after giving birth to Mary. Indeed, some critics have seen the creature's yearning for Victor as emblematic of Mary's own desire for her dead mother.

Demon Lovers and Femme Fatales

The history of the 'demon lover' can be traced back to Assyrian and Babylonian mythology with the creation of Lilith, Adam's first wife. Lilith, having demanded to be treated as an equal, was cast out of the Garden of Eden and subsequently preyed upon Adam, creating her own demon army from his seed. Lilith is briefly mentioned in the Bible, though is often referred to obliquely as the 'night hag' (see Koltuv's *The Book of Lilith* and Bywater's *The Devil's Ark*). Lilith, in keeping with several other female characters in the Bible, encapsulates the demon lover with her sexual prowess and destructive nature.

The protagonist's fall in the gothic genre is, as with the Bible, sometimes accomplished through a relationship with a 'demon lover' who acts as the protagonist's double or alter-ego, leading the protagonist into experiences forbidden by societal norms. The demon lover is frequently female, a femme fatale (fatal or deadly woman) who seduces and entices the protagonist to destruction. While in some cases, the femme fatale seems indicative of the misogyny of patriarchal cultures, in others, the masterful and destroying female seems to enact a fantasy of female empowerment.

In *Northanger Abbey* Isabella Thorpe is the nearest thing to a femme fatale, although she is punished for her waywardness. Austen allows Isabella to say things which are unfeeling and hurtful and in many ways her character acts as a brilliantly executed contrast to Catherine's. Unlike Catherine she is unstable, capricious, self-contradictory and morally blind. Her attempt to gain the Morlands' friendship after breaking her engagement is pathetic and Austen's final judgement is severe: she can no longer be Catherine's friend.

Other females are passive victims, unable to save themselves either from the feelings that they have or the situation they find themselves in. Indeed it is the passive victim with whom the early female reader would have identified with, thus experiencing the vicarious thrill of being ravished without feeling guilty.

Motifs

Temptation and transgression are the central motifs of the gothic. The idea of forbidden fruit, the locked casket, room or house is the clichéd catalyst that still drives the majority of gothic narratives. Either the protagonist actively oversteps the mark or he/she invites the danger into their own, previously safe environment. And, as said earlier, it is curiosity that allows the reader to identify with the protagonist. At the heart of these stories of temptation there is a moral paradox. Surely, it can be argued, the pursuit of knowledge is a positive aspect of human endeavour – it is a fundamental aspect of the human condition and humanity refuses to be denied the answers to any question it might ask no matter how terrible the answer might be. Pushing the limits of knowledge and the consequences of such a search has become part and parcel of the scientific age and, again, this has easily been assimilated into the gothic model.

The forbidden knowledge or Faust motif takes its name from the German legend of Dr Faustus, who sold his soul to the devil to obtain power and knowledge forbidden to ordinary humans. Forbidden knowledge and power is often the gothic protagonist's goal. The gothic 'hero' questions the universe's ambiguous nature and tries to comprehend and control those supernatural powers that mortals cannot understand. He tries to overcome human limitations and make himself into a 'god'. This ambition usually leads to the hero's 'fall' or destruction; however, gothic tales of ambition sometimes paradoxically evoke our admiration because they picture individuals with the courage to defy fate and cosmic forces in an attempt to transcend the mundane to the eternal and sublime. It is also interesting to note that while men strive for knowledge and understanding, women are frequently portrayed as being merely curious.

The persecuted and frequently pursued maiden is another major motif, the idea of somebody defenceless exposed to tyranny and loss. As, of course, is the ghost. Ghosts have never been absent from literature – think, for example, of

Shakespeare's *Hamlet* – but in the gothic we are constantly in the presence of ghosts, or at least of phenomena which might be considered ghostly, even if, as in the case of Radcliffe, they are usually explained away in the final few pages.

Other motifs include the gothic castle, as in Dracula's castle and in works by Walpole, Radcliffe and Carter. The castle is a sinister, forbidding, a place where maidens find themselves persecuted by feudal barons, a reference to a medieval past which somehow remains as the site of our worst fears and terrors.

Then, of course, there is the vampire, who makes his first significant appearance in John Polidori's *The Vampyre* but becomes a source of obsession in much nineteenth-century literature. A particularly interesting example is the lesbian vampire in Sheridan LeFanu's *Carmilla*, although it is Stoker's *Dracula* who has most indelibly fixed himself in the minds of English readers.

And alongside these, there are all manner of monsters – Mary Shelley's is the most obvious – as well as zombies and the walking dead, found in contemporary novels such as *Night of the Damned*. A further, long-lived motif is the double, or doppelganger. *The Strange Case of Dr Jekyll and Mr Hyde* is the most obvious example. The life-or-death experience of discovering, or being discovered by a double, runs right through gothic literature.

Black Humour

If the gothic aims to shock and unsettle, then it is perhaps not too surprising that dark humour, grim irony and an evocation of the grotesque and the ridiculous are an important means by which these aims are achieved. The gothic deals with the extreme, uncanny, supernatural and therefore often teeters on the edge of the absurd – but then this is entirely appropriate for a genre in which nothing is held sacred.

The use of black humour to reinforce gothic themes is also seen in the disillusionment and ironic realisation of characters who have sought to achieve their desires at any cost, only to see them turn to dust. A wry appreciation of the futility of battling against the odds and a recognition of the grotesque ironies of life is evident in the most perceptive of characters in the gothic and concern with the trivial at the expense of the serious is not just funny in itself but helps the writer to point up the importance of seeing clearly the true nature of men and women.

Reading the Gothic

In France, the infamous Marquis de Sade wrote the first major criticism of the gothic, attributing its growth to the dangers and terrors of the French Revolution. Some argue that the gothic is a response to anxieties that the ancient feudal, aristocratic order might return to unsettle bourgeois conventions, a set of conventions which, on the surface, seemed certain of dominance during the eighteenth century but which were, perhaps, not quite as secure as they seemed. Aristocrats are frequently vilified, yet there is also the fear of the mob.

In gothic novels the normal world is rendered void and the reader becomes complicit in whatever he or she might encounter. The vicarious thrill lies in shared act of transgression – the reader is tasting forbidden fruit, opening dangerous boxes in the hope of enjoying the illicit pleasures made available to the protagonist. The narrative often involves journeys into the unknown and this is a metaphorical enactment of the act of 'reading' text itself. The texts themselves are often forbidden; beyond the bounds of acceptable literature and the very act of reading them is, in itself, a flouting of the authority of the legitimate canon of 'worthy texts'. Perhaps it is the darkness within us, the desire for bloodshed or the taboo, which craves what these damned and damning texts contain.

Glossary

Bildungsroman: a formation novel or coming-of-age story; a literary genre that focuses on the psychological and moral growth of the protagonist from youth to adulthood and in which character development is thus extremely important.

Epistolary: an epistolary novel is written as a series of documents. The usual form is letters although diary entries, newspaper clippings and other documents are sometimes used. The epistolary form can add greater realism or verisimilitude to a story, because it mimics the workings of real life. It is thus able to demonstrate differing points of view without recourse to the device of an omniscient narrator. There are three types of epistolary novels: monologic (giving the letters of only one character, like Letters of a Portuguese Nun), dialogic (giving the letters of two characters), and polylogic (with three or more letter-writing characters, such as in Bram Stoker's *Dracula*). In addition, a crucial element in polylogic epistolary novels like *Clarissa*, and *Dangerous Liaisons* is the dramatic device of 'discrepant awareness': the simultaneous but separate correspondences of the heroines and the villains creating dramatic tension.

Eponymous: (adjective) of, relating to, or being the person or entity after which something or someone is named. Tristram Shandy is the eponymous hero of the novel; Othello is the eponymous protagonist of the Shakespearian tragedy *Othello*.

Free indirect discourse or speech: is a third person narrative which uses some of the characteristics of third-person along with the essence of first person direct speech. What distinguishes free indirect discourse or speech from normal indirect speech is the lack of an introductory expression such as 'She said' or 'She thought'. It is as if the subordinate clause carrying the content of the indirect speech is taken out of the main clause. Using free indirect speech may convey the character's words more directly than in normal indirect, as devices such as interjections and exclamation marks can be used that cannot be normally used within a subordinate clause. Jane Austen is cited as one of the first novelists to use this style consistently. Quoted or direct speech: He laid down his bundle and thought of his misfortune. 'And just what pleasure have I found, since I came into this world?' he asked. Reported or normal indirect speech: He laid down his bundle and thought of his misfortune. He asked himself what pleasure he had found since he came into the world. Free indirect speech: He laid down his bundle and thought of his misfortune. And just what pleasure had he found, since he came into this world? Austen's use of free indirect speech is evident in the exclamatory sentence 'Northanger Abbey!', Catherine's unspoken response to her invitation to stay at the eponymous abbey.

Motif: any recurring element that has symbolic significance in a story. Through its repetition, a motif can help produce other narrative (or literary) aspects such as theme or mood. While it may appear interchangeable with the related concept theme the term 'motif' does differ somewhat in usage. Any number of narrative elements with symbolic significance can be classified as motifs - whether they are images, spoken or written phrases, structural or stylistic devices, or other elements like sound, physical movement, or visual components in dramatic narratives. To distinguish between a motif and theme a general rule is that a theme is abstract and a motif is concrete.

Radcliffean: in The Radcliffean Gothic Model: A Form for Feminine Sexuality Cynthia Wolff addresses sexuality in gothic novels and how women have to deal with the 'virgin/whore' syndrome. It is also interesting to note that while women fall into the category of virgin/whore, men fall into the category of villains and/or heroes. Wolff writes, 'The heroine becomes 'somebody' when she is united with such a man. Marriage seals the bargain by which she becomes mistress of the castle.' Within Northanger Abbey Catherine eagerly casts General Tilney as the Radcliffean villain.

Southern Gothic: combines some gothic sensibilities (such as the grotesque) with the setting and style of the Southern United States. Examples include William Faulkner and Poppy Z Brite.

Suburban Gothic: a subgenre of gothic fiction, film and television, focused on anxieties associated with the creation of suburban communities, particularly in the United States, from the 1950s and 1960s onwards. It often, but not exclusively, relies on the supernatural but manifested in a suburban setting; an early example being Ira Levin's *Rosemary's Baby.*

A List of Gothic Novels and Short Stories

Frankenstein – Mary Shelley, 1818
Northanger Abbey – Jane Austen, 1818
The Tell-Tale Heart – Edgar Allan Poe, 1843
Jane Eyre - Charlotte Brontë, 1847
Wuthering Heights – Emily Brontë, 1847
The Mystery of Edwin Drood – Charles Dickens, 1870
The Strange Case of Dr Jekyll and Mr Hyde – Robert Louis Stevenson, 1886
The Beetle – Richard Marsh, 1897
Dracula – Bram Stoker, 1897
The Rats in the Walls – H.P. Lovecraft, 1923
Rebecca – Daphne du Maurier, 1938
Rosemary's Baby – Ira Levin, 1967
The Shining – Stephen King, 1977
The Bloody Chamber – 1977, Angela Carter
Interview with a Vampire – Anne Rice, 1977
Bellefleur – Joyce Carol Oates, 1980
Lost Souls – Poppy Z Brite, 1992
House of Leaves – Mark Z Danielewski, 2000
Floating Staircase – Ronald Malfi, 2011
Night of the Damned – Stephen Bywater, 2015

Further Critical Reading

Gothic Horror: A Critical Anthology - Clive Bloom, 1998
Gothic, the New Critical Idiom – Fred Botting, 1996
Nightmare: Birth of Horror - Christopher Frayling, 1996
Love, Mystery and Misery: Feeling in Gothic Fiction - Coral Ann Howells, 1978
The Radcliffean Gothic Model: A Form of Feminine Sexuality - Modern Language Studies - Cynthia Griffin Wolff, 1979
The Literature of Terror: A History of Gothic Fiction from 1765 to the Present Day - David Punter 1980

Excerpts from Northanger Abbey

The carefully selected excerpts which follow are included for revision. They will allow you to focus on gothic aspects within the novel without having to search through or re-read the whole text. Critical comments are included at the end of each chapter.

ADVERTISEMENT BY THE AUTHORESS, TO NORTHANGER ABBEY

THIS little work was finished in the year 1803, and intended for immediate publication. It was disposed of to a bookseller, it was even advertised, and why the business proceeded no farther, the author has never been able to learn. That any bookseller should think it worth-while to purchase what he did not think it worth-while to publish seems extraordinary. But with this, neither the author nor the public have any other concern than as some observation is necessary upon those parts of the work which thirteen years have made comparatively obsolete. The public are entreated to bear in mind that thirteen years have passed since it was finished, many more since it was begun, and that during that period, places, manners, books, and opinions have undergone considerable changes.

CHAPTER 1

No one who had ever seen Catherine Morland in her infancy would have supposed her born to be an heroine. Her situation in life, the character of her father and mother, her own person and disposition, were all equally against her. Her father was a clergyman, without being neglected, or poor, and a very respectable man, though his name was Richard and he had never been handsome. He had a considerable independence besides two good livings and he was not in the least addicted to locking up his daughters. Her mother was a woman of useful plain sense, with a good temper, and, what is more remarkable, with a good constitution. She had three sons before Catherine was born; and instead of dying in bringing the latter into the world, as anybody might expect, she still lived on lived to have six children more to see them growing up around her, and to enjoy excellent health herself. A family of ten children will be always called a fine family, where there are heads and arms and legs enough for the number; but the Morlands had little other right to the word, for they were in general very plain, and Catherine, for many years of her life, as plain as any. She had a thin awkward figure, a sallow skin without colour, dark lank hair, and strong features so much for her person; and not less unpropitious for heroism seemed her mind. She was fond of all boy's plays, and greatly preferred cricket not merely to dolls, but to the more heroic enjoyments of infancy, nursing a dormouse, feeding a canary-bird, or watering a rose-bush. Indeed she had no taste for a garden; and if she gathered flowers at all, it was chiefly for the pleasure of mischief at least so it was conjectured from her always preferring those which she was forbidden to take. Such were her propensities her abilities were quite as extraordinary. She never could learn or understand anything before she was taught; and sometimes not even then, for she was often inattentive, and occasionally stupid. Her mother was three months in teaching her only to repeat the 'Beggar's Petition'; and after all, her next sister, Sally, could say it better than she did. Not that Catherine was always stupid by no means; she learnt the fable of 'The Hare and Many Friends' as quickly as any girl in England. Her mother wished her to learn music; and Catherine was sure she should like it, for she was very fond of tinkling the keys of the old forlorn spinnet; so, at eight years old she began. She learnt a year, and could not bear it; and Mrs. Morland, who did not insist on her daughters being accomplished in spite of incapacity or distaste, allowed her to leave off. The day which dismissed the music-master was one of the happiest of Catherine's life. Her taste for drawing was not superior; though whenever she could obtain the outside of a letter from her mother or seize upon any other odd piece of paper, she did what she could in that way, by drawing houses and trees, hens and chickens, all very much like one another. Writing and accounts she was taught by her father; French by her mother: her proficiency in either was not remarkable, and she shirked her lessons in both whenever she could. What a strange, unaccountable character! for with all these symptoms of profligacy at ten years old, she had neither a bad heart nor a bad temper, was seldom stubborn, scarcely ever quarrelsome, and very kind to the little ones, with few interruptions of tyranny; she was moreover noisy and wild, hated confinement and cleanliness, and loved nothing so well in the world as rolling down the green slope at the back of the house.

Such was Catherine Morland at ten. At fifteen, appearances were mending; she began to curl her hair and long for balls; her complexion improved, her features were softened by plumpness and colour, her eyes gained more animation, and her figure more consequence. Her love of dirt gave way to an inclination for finery, and she grew clean as she grew smart; she had now the pleasure of sometimes hearing her father and mother remark on her personal improvement. 'Catherine grows quite a good-looking girl she is almost pretty today,' were words which caught her ears now and then; and how welcome were the sounds! To look almost pretty is an acquisition of higher delight to a girl who has been looking plain the first fifteen years of her life than a beauty from her cradle can ever receive.

Mrs. Morland was a very good woman, and wished to see her children everything they ought to be; but her time was so much occupied in lying-in and teaching the little ones, that her elder daughters were inevitably left to shift for themselves; and it was not very wonderful that Catherine, who had by nature nothing heroic about her, should prefer cricket, baseball, riding on horseback, and running about the country at the age of fourteen, to books or at least books of information for, provided that nothing like useful knowledge could be gained from them, provided they were all story and no reflection, she had never any objection to books at all. But from fifteen to seventeen she was in training for a heroine; she read all such works as heroines must read to supply their memories with those quotations which are so serviceable and so soothing in the vicissitudes of their eventful lives.

From Pope, she learnt to censure those who 'bear about the mockery of woe.'

From Gray, that 'Many a flower is born to blush unseen, And waste its fragrance on the desert air.'

From Thompson, that 'It is a delightful task to teach the young idea how to shoot.'

And from Shakespeare she gained a great store of information amongst the rest, that 'Trifles light as air, Are, to the jealous, confirmation strong, As proofs of Holy Writ.'

That 'The poor beetle, which we tread upon, In corporal sufferance feels a pang as great As when a giant dies.'

And that a young woman in love always looks like 'Patience on a monument Smiling at Grief.'

So far her improvement was sufficient and in many other points she came on exceedingly well; for though she could not write sonnets, she brought herself to read them; and though there seemed no chance of her throwing a whole party into raptures by a prelude on the pianoforte, of her own composition, she could listen to other people's performance with very little fatigue. Her greatest deficiency was in the pencil she had no notion of drawing not enough even to attempt a sketch of her lover's profile, that she might be detected in the design. There she fell miserably short of the true heroic height. At present she did not know her own poverty, for she had no lover to portray. She had reached the age of seventeen, without having seen one amiable youth who could call forth her sensibility, without having inspired one real passion, and without having excited even any admiration but what was very moderate and very transient. This was strange indeed! But strange things may be generally accounted for if their cause be fairly searched out. There was not one lord in the neighbourhood; no not even a baronet. There was not one family among their acquaintance who had reared and supported a boy accidentally found at their door not one young man whose origin was unknown. Her father had no ward, and the squire of the parish no children.

But when a young lady is to be a heroine, the perverseness of forty surrounding families cannot prevent her. Something must and will happen to throw a hero in her way.

Mr. Allen, who owned the chief of the property about Fullerton, the village in Wiltshire where the Morlands lived, was ordered to Bath for the benefit of a gouty constitution and his lady, a good-humoured woman, fond of Miss Morland, and probably aware that if adventures will not befall a young lady in her own village, she must seek them abroad, invited her to go with them. Mr. and Mrs. Morland were all compliance, and Catherine all happiness.

Note: Catherine hardly seems fit to be a heroine and her parents are very ordinary people. However, 'from fifteen to seventeen she was in training for a heroine'. The three quotations from Shakespeare are in keeping with her idea of herself as a potential heroine and convey her strong imagination, her desired sensitivity and readiness to suffer.

CHAPTER 2

Sally, or rather Sarah (for what young lady of common gentility will reach the age of sixteen without altering her name as far as she can?), must from situation be at this time the intimate friend and confidante of her sister. It is remarkable, however, that she neither insisted on Catherine's writing by every post, nor exacted her promise of transmitting the character of every new acquaintance, nor a detail of every interesting conversation that Bath might produce. Everything indeed relative to this important journey was done, on the part of the Morlands, with a degree of moderation and composure, which seemed rather consistent with the common feelings of common life, than with the refined susceptibilities, the tender emotions which the first separation of a heroine from her family ought always to excite. Her father, instead of giving her an unlimited order on his banker, or even putting an hundred pounds bank-bill into her hands, gave her only ten guineas, and promised her more when she wanted it.

Under these unpromising auspices, the parting took place, and the journey began. It was performed with suitable quietness and uneventful safety. Neither robbers nor tempests befriended them, nor one lucky overturn to introduce them to the hero. Nothing more alarming occurred than a fear, on Mrs. Allen's side, of having once left her clogs behind her at an inn, and that fortunately proved to be groundless.

Yet Catherine was in very good looks, and had the company only seen her three years before, they would now have thought her exceedingly handsome.

She was looked at, however, and with some admiration; for, in her own hearing, two gentlemen pronounced her to be a pretty girl. Such words had their due effect; she immediately thought the evening pleasanter than she had found it before her humble vanity was contented she felt more obliged to the two young men for this simple praise than a true-quality heroine would have been for fifteen sonnets in celebration of her charms, and went to her chair in good humour with everybody, and perfectly satisfied with her share of public attention.

Note: after an uneventful journey with no 'lucky overturn' (an overturned carriage in romantic novels became a common way to introduce the heroine to the hero) Catherine and the Allens arrive in Bath.

CHAPTER 3

They made their appearance in the Lower Rooms; and here fortune was more favourable to our heroine. The master of the ceremonies introduced to her a very gentlemanlike young man as a partner; his name was Tilney. He seemed to be about four or five and twenty, was rather tall, had a pleasing countenance, a very intelligent and lively eye, and, if not quite handsome, was very near it. His address was good, and Catherine felt herself in high luck. There was little leisure for speaking while they danced; but when they were seated at tea, she found him as agreeable as she had already given him credit for being. He talked with fluency and spirit and there was an archness and pleasantry in his manner which interested, though it was hardly understood by her.

Note: a routine is quickly established. Austen makes reference to Samuel Richardson, author of *Pamela* (1740) and one of Austen's favourite writers.

CHAPTER 4

'Here come my dear girls,' cried Mrs. Thorpe, pointing at three smart-looking females who, arm in arm, were then moving towards her. 'My dear Mrs. Allen, I long to introduce them; they will be so delighted to see you: the tallest is Isabella, my eldest; is not she a fine young woman? The others are very much admired too, but I believe Isabella is the handsomest.'

The Miss Thorpes were introduced; and Miss Morland, who had been for a short time forgotten, was introduced likewise. The name seemed to strike them all; and, after speaking to her with great civility, the eldest young lady observed aloud to the rest, 'How excessively like her brother Miss Morland is!'

'The very picture of him indeed!' cried the mother and 'I should have known her anywhere for his sister!' was repeated by them all, two or three times over. For a moment Catherine was surprised; but Mrs. Thorpe and her daughters had scarcely begun the history of their acquaintance with Mr. James Morland, before she remembered that her eldest brother had lately formed an intimacy with a young man of his own college, of the name of Thorpe; and that he had spent the last week of the Christmas vacation with his family, near London.

Catherine was delighted with this extension of her Bath acquaintance, and almost forgot Mr. Tilney while she talked to Miss Thorpe. Friendship is certainly the finest balm for the pangs of disappointed love.

Their conversation turned upon those subjects, of which the free discussion has generally much to do in perfecting a sudden intimacy between two young ladies: such as dress, balls, flirtations, and quizzes. Miss Thorpe, however, being four years older than Miss Morland, and at least four years better informed, had a very decided advantage in discussing such points; she could compare the balls of Bath with those of Tunbridge, its fashions with the fashions of London; could rectify the opinions of her new friend in many articles of tasteful attire; could discover a flirtation between any gentleman and lady who only smiled on each other; and point out a quiz through the thickness of a crowd. These powers received due admiration from Catherine, to whom they were entirely new; and the respect which they naturally inspired might have been too great for familiarity, had not the easy gaiety of Miss Thorpe's manners, and her frequent expressions of delight on this acquaintance with her, softened down every feeling of awe, and left nothing but tender affection.

Note: Catherine and Isabella become firm friends. Tunbridge Wells is a spa town in Kent.

CHAPTER 5

The progress of the friendship between Catherine and Isabella was quick as its beginning had been warm, and they passed so rapidly through every gradation of increasing tenderness that there was shortly no fresh proof of it to be given to their friends or themselves. They called each other by their Christian name, were always arm in arm when they walked, pinned up each other's train for the dance, and were not to be divided in the set; and if a rainy morning deprived them of other enjoyments, they were still resolute in meeting in defiance of wet and dirt, and shut themselves up, to read novels together. Yes, novels; for I will not adopt that ungenerous and impolitic custom so common with novel-writers, of degrading by their contemptuous censure the very performances, to the number of which they are themselves adding joining with their greatest enemies in bestowing the harshest epithets on such works, and scarcely ever permitting them to be read by their own heroine, who, if she accidentally take up a novel, is sure to turn over its insipid pages with disgust. Alas! If the heroine of one novel be not patronized by the heroine of another, from whom can she expect protection and regard? I cannot approve of it. Let us leave it to the reviewers to abuse such effusions of fancy at their leisure, and over every new novel to talk in threadbare strains of the trash with which the press now groans. Let us not desert one another; we are an injured body. Although our productions have afforded more extensive and unaffected pleasure than those of any other literary corporation in the world, no species of composition has been so much decried. From pride, ignorance, or fashion, our foes are almost as many as our readers. And while the abilities of the nine-hundredth abridger of the History of England, or of the man who collects and publishes in a volume some dozen lines of Milton, Pope, and Prior, with a paper from the Spectator, and a chapter from Sterne, are eulogized by a thousand pens there seems almost a general wish of decrying the capacity and undervaluing the labour of the novelist, and of slighting the performances which have only genius, wit, and taste to recommend them. 'I am no novel-reader I seldom look into novels Do not imagine that I often read novels It is really very well for a novel.' Such is the common cant. 'And what are you reading, Miss ?' 'Oh! It is only a novel!' replies the young lady, while she lays down her book with affected indifference, or momentary shame. 'It is only *Cecilia*, or *Camilla,* or *Belinda*'; or, in short, only some work in which the greatest powers of the mind are displayed, in which the most thorough knowledge of human nature, the happiest delineation of its varieties, the liveliest effusions of wit and humour, are conveyed to the world in the best-chosen language. Now, had the same young lady been engaged with a volume of the Spectator, instead of such a work, how proudly would she have produced the book, and told its name; though the chances must be against her being occupied by any part of that voluminous publication, of which either the matter or manner would not disgust a young person of taste: the substance of its papers so often consisting in the statement of improbable circumstances, unnatural characters, and topics of conversation which no longer concern anyone living; and their language, too, frequently so coarse as to give no very favourable idea of the age that could endure it.

Note: Mrs Allen is happy having met the Thorpes. Catherine and Isabella begin to discuss novels with reference to *Cecilia* and *Camilla* (both written by Fanny Burney, 1752-1840) and *Belinda* (Maria Edgeworth, 1767-1849).

CHAPTER 6

They met by appointment; and as Isabella had arrived nearly five minutes before her friend, her first address naturally was, 'My dearest creature, what can have made you so late? I have been waiting for you at least this age!'

'Have you, indeed! I am very sorry for it; but really I thought I was in very good time. It is but just one. I hope you have not been here long?'

'Oh! These ten ages at least. I am sure I have been here this half hour. But now, let us go and sit down at the other end of the room, and enjoy ourselves. I have an hundred things to say to you. In the first place, I was so afraid it would rain this morning, just as I wanted to set off; it looked very showery, and that would have thrown me into agonies! Do you know, I saw the prettiest hat you can imagine, in a shop window in Milsom Street just now very like yours, only with coquelicot ribbons instead of green; I quite longed for it. But, my dearest Catherine, what have you been doing with yourself all this morning? Have you gone on with *Udolpho*?'

'Yes, I have been reading it ever since I woke; and I am got to the black veil.'

'Are you, indeed? How delightful! Oh! I would not tell you what is behind the black veil for the world! Are not you wild to know?'

'Oh! Yes, quite; what can it be? But do not tell me I would not be told upon any account. I know it must be a skeleton, I am sure it is Laurentina's skeleton. Oh! I am delighted with the book! I should like to spend my whole life in reading it. I assure you, if it had not been to meet you, I would not have come away from it for all the world.'

'Dear creature! How much I am obliged to you; and when you have finished *Udolpho*, we will read the Italian together; and I have made out a list of ten or twelve more of the same kind for you.'

'Have you, indeed! How glad I am! What are they all?'

'I will read you their names directly; here they are, in my pocketbook. Castle of Wolfenbach, Clermont, Mysterious Warnings, Necromancer of the Black Forest, Midnight Bell, Orphan of the Rhine, and Horrid Mysteries. Those will last us some time.'

'Yes, pretty well; but are they all horrid, are you sure they are all horrid?'

'Yes, quite sure; for a particular friend of mine, a Miss Andrews, a sweet girl, one of the sweetest creatures in the world, has read every one of them. I wish you knew Miss Andrews, you would be delighted with her. She is netting herself the sweetest cloak you can conceive. I think her as beautiful as an angel, and I am so vexed with the men for not admiring her! I scold them all amazingly about it.'

'Scold them! Do you scold them for not admiring her?'

'Yes, that I do. There is nothing I would not do for those who are really my friends. I have no notion of loving people by halves; it is not my nature. My attachments are always excessively strong. I told Captain Hunt at one of our assemblies this winter that if he was to tease me all night, I would not dance with him, unless he would allow Miss Andrews to be as beautiful as an angel. The men think us incapable of real friendship, you know, and I am determined to show them the difference. Now, if I were to hear anybody speak slightingly of you, I should fire up in a moment: but that is not at all likely, for you are just the kind of girl to be a great favourite with the men.'

'Oh, dear!' cried Catherine, colouring. 'How can you say so?'

'I know you very well; you have so much animation, which is exactly what Miss Andrews wants, for I must confess there is something amazingly insipid about her. Oh! I must tell you, that just after we parted yesterday, I saw a young man looking at you so earnestly I am sure he is in love with you.' Catherine coloured, and disclaimed again. Isabella laughed. 'It is very true, upon my honour, but I see how it is; you are indifferent to everybody's admiration, except that of one gentleman, who shall be nameless. Nay, I cannot blame you' speaking more seriously 'your feelings are easily understood. Where the heart is really attached, I know very well how little one can be pleased with the attention of anybody else. Everything is so insipid, so uninteresting, that does not relate to the beloved object! I can perfectly comprehend your feelings.'

'But you should not persuade me that I think so very much about Mr. Tilney, for perhaps I may never see him again.'

'Not see him again! My dearest creature, do not talk of it. I am sure you would be miserable if you thought so!'

'No, indeed, I should not. I do not pretend to say that I was not very much pleased with him; but while I have *Udolpho* to read, I feel as if nobody could make me miserable. Oh! The dreadful black veil! My dear Isabella, I am sure there must be Laurentina's skeleton behind it.'

'It is so odd to me, that you should never have read *Udolpho* before; but I suppose Mrs. Morland objects to novels.'

'No, she does not. She very often reads *Sir Charles Grandison* [an early epistolary novel by Samuel Richardson] herself; but new books do not fall in our way.'

'*Sir Charles Grandison*! That is an amazing horrid book, is it not? I remember Miss Andrews could not get through the first volume.'

'It is not like *Udolpho* at all; but yet I think it is very entertaining.'

'Do you indeed! You surprise me; I thought it had not been readable. But, my dearest Catherine, have you settled what to wear on your head tonight? I am determined at all events to be dressed exactly like you. The men take notice of that sometimes, you know.'

'But it does not signify if they do,' said Catherine, very innocently.

'Signify! Oh, heavens! I make it a rule never to mind what they say. They are very often amazingly impertinent if you do not treat them with spirit, and make them keep their distance.'

'Are they? Well, I never observed that. They always behave very well to me.'

'Oh! They give themselves such airs. They are the most conceited creatures in the world, and think themselves of so much importance! By the by, though I have thought of it a hundred times, I have always forgot to ask you what is your favourite complexion in a man. Do you like them best dark or fair?'

'I hardly know. I never much thought about it. Something between both, I think. Brown not fair, and and not very dark.'

'Very well, Catherine. That is exactly he. I have not forgot your description of Mr. Tilney 'a brown skin, with dark eyes, and rather dark hair.' Well, my taste is different. I prefer light eyes, and as to complexion do you know I like a sallow better than any other. You must not betray me, if you should ever meet with one of your acquaintance answering that description.'

'Betray you! What do you mean?'

'Nay, do not distress me. I believe I have said too much. Let us drop the subject.'

Catherine, in some amazement, complied, and after remaining a few moments silent, was on the point of reverting to what interested her at that time rather more than anything else in the world, Laurentina's skeleton, when her friend prevented her, by saying, 'For heaven's sake! Let us move away from this end of the room. Do you know, there are two odious young men who have been staring at me this half hour. They really put me quite out of countenance. Let us go and look at the arrivals. They will hardly follow us there.'

Note: Isabella's enjoyment of 'horrid' novels and her familiarity with the gothic genre. All the titles mentioned are genuine as is the episode with the 'black veil'.

CHAPTER 7

John Thorpe, who in the meantime had been giving orders about the horses, soon joined them, and from him she directly received the amends which were her due; for while he slightly and carelessly touched the hand of Isabella, on her he bestowed a whole scrape and half a short bow. He was a stout young man of middling height, who, with a plain face and ungraceful form, seemed fearful of being too handsome unless he wore the dress of a groom, and too much like a gentleman unless he were easy where he ought to be civil, and impudent where he might be allowed to be easy. He took out his watch: 'How long do you think we have been running it from Tetbury, Miss Morland?'

'I do not know the distance.' Her brother told her that it was twenty-three miles.

'Three and twenty!' cried Thorpe. 'Five and twenty if it is an inch.' Morland remonstrated, pleaded the authority of road-books, innkeepers, and milestones; but his friend disregarded them all; he had a surer test of distance. 'I know it must be five and twenty,' said he, 'by the time we have been doing it. It is now half after one; we drove out of the inn-yard at Tetbury as the town clock struck eleven; and I defy any man in England to make my horse go less than ten miles an hour in harness; that makes it exactly twenty-five.'

This brought on a dialogue of civilities between the other two; but Catherine heard neither the particulars nor the result. Her companion's discourse now sunk from its hitherto animated pitch to nothing more than a short decisive sentence of praise or condemnation on the face of every woman they met; and Catherine, after listening and agreeing as long as she could, with all the civility and deference of the youthful female mind, fearful of hazarding an opinion of its own in opposition to that of a self-assured man, especially where the beauty of her own sex is concerned, ventured at length to vary the subject by a question which had been long uppermost in her thoughts; it was, 'Have you ever read *Udolpho*, Mr. Thorpe?'

'*Udolpho*! Oh, Lord! Not I; I never read novels; I have something else to do.'

Catherine, humbled and ashamed, was going to apologize for her question, but he prevented her by saying, 'Novels are all so full of nonsense and stuff; there has not been a tolerably decent one come out since *Tom Jones*, except *The Monk*; I read that t'other day; but as for all the others, they are the stupidest things in creation.'

'I think you must like *Udolpho*, if you were to read it; it is so very interesting.'

'Not I, faith! No, if I read any, it shall be Mrs. Radcliffe's; her novels are amusing enough; they are worth reading; some fun and nature in them.'

'*Udolpho* was written by Mrs. Radcliffe,' said Catherine, with some hesitation, from the fear of mortifying him.

'No sure; was it? Aye, I remember, so it was; I was thinking of that other stupid book, written by that woman they make such a fuss about, she who married the French emigrant.'

'I suppose you mean Camilla?'

'Yes, that's the book; such unnatural stuff! An old man playing at see-saw, I took up the first volume once and looked it over, but I soon found it would not do; indeed I guessed what sort of stuff it must be before I saw it: as soon as I heard she had married an emigrant, I was sure I should never be able to get through it.'

'I have never read it.'

'You had no loss, I assure you; it is the horridest nonsense you can imagine; there is nothing in the world in it but an old man's playing at see-saw and learning Latin; upon my soul there is not.'

This critique, the justness of which was unfortunately lost on poor Catherine, brought them to the door of Mrs. Thorpe's lodgings, and the feelings of the discerning and unprejudiced reader of Camilla gave way to the feelings of the dutiful and affectionate son, as they met Mrs. Thorpe, who had descried them from above, in the passage. 'Ah, Mother! How do you do?' said he, giving her a hearty shake of the hand. 'Where did you get that quiz of a hat? It makes you look like an old witch. Here is Morland and I come to stay a few days with you, so you must look out for a couple of good beds somewhere near.' And this address seemed to satisfy all the fondest wishes of the mother's heart, for she received him with the most delighted and exulting affection. On his two younger sisters he then bestowed an equal portion of his fraternal tenderness, for he asked each of them how they did, and observed that they both looked very ugly.

James accepted this tribute of gratitude, and qualified his conscience for accepting it too, by saying with perfect sincerity, 'Indeed, Catherine, I love you dearly.'

Inquiries and communications concerning brothers and sisters, the situation of some, the growth of the rest, and other family matters now passed between them, and continued, with only one small digression on James's part, in praise of Miss

Thorpe, till they reached Pulteney Street, where he was welcomed with great kindness by Mr. and Mrs. Allen, invited by the former to dine with them, and summoned by the latter to guess the price and weigh the merits of a new muff and tippet. A pre-engagement in Edgar's Buildings prevented his accepting the invitation of one friend, and obliged him to hurry away as soon as he had satisfied the demands of the other. The time of the two parties uniting in the Octagon Room being correctly adjusted, Catherine was then left to the luxury of a raised, restless, and frightened imagination over the pages of *Udolpho*, lost from all worldly concerns of dressing and dinner, incapable of soothing Mrs. Allen's fears on the delay of an expected dressmaker, and having only one minute in sixty to bestow even on the reflection of her own felicity, in being already engaged for the evening.

Note: *The Monk* is another gothic novel (M.G. Lewis, 1796). John Thorpe's taste in books is rather coarse and conveys a limited understanding of literature.

CHAPTER 11

'You croaking fellow!' cried Thorpe. 'We shall be able to do ten times more. Kingsweston! Aye, and Blaize Castle too, and anything else we can hear of; but here is your sister says she will not go.'

'Blaize Castle!' cried Catherine. 'What is that?'

'The finest place in England worth going fifty miles at any time to see.'

'What, is it really a castle, an old castle?'

'The oldest in the kingdom.'

'But is it like what one reads of?'

'Exactly the very same.'

'But now really are there towers and long galleries?'

'By dozens.'

'Then I should like to see it; but I cannot I cannot go.

It was now but an hour later than the time fixed on for the beginning of their walk; and, in spite of what she had heard of the prodigious accumulation of dirt in the course of that hour, she could not from her own observation help thinking that they might have gone with very little inconvenience. To feel herself slighted by them was very painful. On the other hand, the delight of exploring an edifice like Udolpho, as her fancy represented Blaize Castle to be, was such a counterpoise of good as might console her for almost anything.

Their drive, even when this subject was over, was not likely to be very agreeable. Catherine's complaisance was no longer what it had been in their former airing. She listened reluctantly, and her replies were short. Blaize Castle remained her only comfort; towards that, she still looked at intervals with pleasure; though rather than be disappointed of the promised walk, and especially rather than be thought ill of by the Tilneys, she would willingly have given up all the happiness which its walls could supply the happiness of a progress through a long suite of lofty rooms, exhibiting the remains of magnificent furniture, though now for many years deserted the happiness of being stopped in their way along narrow, winding vaults, by a low, grated door; or even of having their lamp, their only lamp, extinguished by a sudden gust of wind, and of being left in total darkness.

Note: Blaize Castle is not the 'oldest in the kingdom', but a folly built in 1771. The description John Thorpe gives is clearly inaccurate.

CHAPTER 14

The Tilneys called for her at the appointed time; and no new difficulty arising, no sudden recollection, no unexpected summons, no impertinent intrusion to disconcert their measures, my heroine was most unnaturally able to fulfil her engagement, though it was made with the hero himself.

They determined on walking round Beechen Cliff, that noble hill whose beautiful verdure and hanging coppice render it so striking an object from almost every opening in Bath.

'I never look at it,' said Catherine, as they walked along the side of the river, 'without thinking of the south of France.'

'You have been abroad then?' said Henry, a little surprised.

'Oh! No, I only mean what I have read about. It always puts me in mind of the country that Emily and her father travelled through, in *The Mysteries of Udolpho*. But you never read novels, I dare say?'

'Why not?'

'Because they are not clever enough for you gentlemen read better books.'

'The person, be it gentleman or lady, who has not pleasure in a good novel, must be intolerably stupid. I have read all Mrs. Radcliffe's works, and most of them with great pleasure. *The Mysteries of Udolpho*, when I had once begun it, I could not lay down again; I remember finishing it in two days my hair standing on end the whole time.'

'Yes,' added Miss Tilney, 'and I remember that you undertook to read it aloud to me, and that when I was called away for only five minutes to answer a note, instead of waiting for me, you took the volume into the Hermitage Walk, and I was obliged to stay till you had finished it.'

'Thank you, Eleanor a most honourable testimony. You see, Miss Morland, the injustice of your suspicions. Here was I, in my eagerness to get on, refusing to wait only five minutes for my sister, breaking the promise I had made of reading it aloud, and keeping her in suspense at a most interesting part, by running away with the volume, which, you are to observe, was her own, particularly her own. I am proud when I reflect on it, and I think it must establish me in your good opinion.'

'I am very glad to hear it indeed, and now I shall never be ashamed of liking *Udolpho* myself. But I really thought before, young men despised novels amazingly.'

'It is amazingly; it may well suggest amazement if they do for they read nearly as many as women. I myself have read hundreds and hundreds. Do not imagine that you can cope with me in a knowledge of Julias and Louisas. If we proceed to particulars, and engage in the never-ceasing inquiry of 'Have you read this?' and 'Have you read that?' I shall soon leave you as far behind me as what shall I say? I want an appropriate simile. as far as your friend Emily herself left poor Valancourt when she went with her aunt into Italy. Consider how many years I have had the start of you. I had entered on my studies at Oxford, while you were a good little girl working your sampler at home!'

'Not very good, I am afraid. But now really, do not you think *Udolpho* the nicest book in the world?'

'The nicest by which I suppose you mean the neatest. That must depend upon the binding.'

'Henry,' said Miss Tilney, 'you are very impertinent. Miss Morland, he is treating you exactly as he does his sister. He is forever finding fault with me, for some incorrectness of language, and now he is taking the same liberty with you. The word 'nicest,' as you used it, did not suit him; and you had better change it as soon as you can, or we shall be overpowered with Johnson and Blair all the rest of the way.'

'I am sure,' cried Catherine, 'I did not mean to say anything wrong; but it is a nice book, and why should not I call it so?'

'Very true,' said Henry, 'and this is a very nice day, and we are taking a very nice walk, and you are two very nice young ladies. Oh! It is a very nice word indeed! It does for everything. Originally perhaps it was applied only to express neatness, propriety, delicacy, or refinement people were nice in their dress, in their sentiments, or their choice. But now every commendation on every subject is comprised in that one word.'

'While, in fact,' cried his sister, 'it ought only to be applied to you, without any commendation at all. You are more nice than wise. Come, Miss Morland, let us leave him to meditate over our faults in the utmost propriety of diction, while we praise Udolpho in whatever terms we like best. It is a most interesting work. You are fond of that kind of reading?'

'To say the truth, I do not much like any other.'

'Indeed!'

'That is, I can read poetry and plays, and things of that sort, and do not dislike travels. But history, real solemn history, I cannot be interested in. Can you?'

'Yes, I am fond of history.'

'I wish I were too. I read it a little as a duty, but it tells me nothing that does not either vex or weary me. The quarrels of popes and kings, with wars or pestilences, in every page; the men all so good for nothing, and hardly any women at all it is very tiresome: and yet I often think it odd that it should be so dull, for a great deal of it must be invention. The speeches that are put into the heroes' mouths, their thoughts and designs the chief of all this must be invention, and invention is what delights me in other books.'

'Historians, you think,' said Miss Tilney, 'are not happy in their flights of fancy. They display imagination without raising interest. I am fond of history and am very well contented to take the false with the true. In the principal facts they have sources of intelligence in former histories and records, which may be as much depended on, I conclude, as anything that does not actually pass under one's own observation; and as for the little embellishments you speak of, they are embellishments, and I like them as such. If a speech be well drawn up, I read it with pleasure, by whomsoever it may be made and probably with much greater, if the production of Mr. Hume or Mr. Robertson, than if the genuine words of Caractacus, Agricola, or Alfred the Great.'

'You are fond of history! And so are Mr. Allen and my father; and I have two brothers who do not dislike it. So many instances within my small circle of friends is remarkable! At this rate, I shall not pity the writers of history any longer. If people like to read their books, it is all very well, but to be at so much trouble in filling great volumes, which, as I used to think, nobody would willingly ever look into, to be labouring only for the torment of little boys and girls, always struck me as a hard fate; and though I know it is all very right and necessary, I have often wondered at the person's courage that could sit down on purpose to do it.'

'That little boys and girls should be tormented,' said Henry, 'is what no one at all acquainted with human nature in a civilized state can deny; but in behalf of our most distinguished historians, I must observe that they might well be offended at being supposed to have no higher aim, and that by their method and style, they are perfectly well qualified to torment readers of the most advanced reason and mature time of life. I use the verb 'to torment,' as I observed to be your own method, instead of 'to instruct,' supposing them to be now admitted as synonymous.'

'You think me foolish to call instruction a torment, but if you had been as much used as myself to hear poor little children first learning their letters and then learning to spell, if you had ever seen how stupid they can be for a whole morning together, and how tired my poor mother is at the end of it, as I am in the habit of seeing almost every day of my life at home, you would allow that 'to torment' and 'to instruct' might sometimes be used as synonymous words.'

'Very probably. But historians are not accountable for the difficulty of learning to read; and even you yourself, who do not altogether seem particularly friendly to very severe, very intense application, may perhaps be brought to acknowledge that it is very well worth-while to be tormented for two or three years of one's life, for the sake of being able to read all the rest of it. Consider if reading had not been taught, Mrs. Radcliffe would have written in vain or perhaps might not have written at all.'

Catherine assented and a very warm panegyric from her on that lady's merits closed the subject.

The general pause which succeeded his short disquisition on the state of the nation was put an end to by Catherine, who, in rather a solemn tone of voice, uttered these words, 'I have heard that something very shocking indeed will soon come out in London.'

Miss Tilney, to whom this was chiefly addressed, was startled, and hastily replied, 'Indeed! And of what nature?'

'That I do not know, nor who is the author. I have only heard that it is to be more horrible than anything we have met with yet.'

'Good heaven! Where could you hear of such a thing?'

'A particular friend of mine had an account of it in a letter from London yesterday. It is to be uncommonly dreadful. I shall expect murder and everything of the kind.'

'You speak with astonishing composure! But I hope your friend's accounts have been exaggerated; and if such a design is known beforehand, proper measures will undoubtedly be taken by government to prevent its coming to effect.'

'Government,' said Henry, endeavouring not to smile, 'neither desires nor dares to interfere in such matters. There must be murder; and government cares not how much.'

The ladies stared. He laughed, and added, 'Come, shall I make you understand each other, or leave you to puzzle out an explanation as you can? No I will be noble. I will prove myself a man, no less by the generosity of my soul than the clearness of my head. I have no patience with such of my sex as disdain to let themselves sometimes down to the comprehension of yours. Perhaps the abilities of women are neither sound nor acute neither vigorous nor keen. Perhaps they may want observation, discernment, judgment, fire, genius, and wit.'

'Miss Morland, do not mind what he says; but have the goodness to satisfy me as to this dreadful riot.'

'Riot! What riot?'

'My dear Eleanor, the riot is only in your own brain. The confusion there is scandalous. Miss Morland has been talking of nothing more dreadful than a new publication which is shortly to come out, in three duodecimo volumes, two hundred and seventy-six pages in each, with a frontispiece to the first, of two tombstones and a lantern do you understand? And you, Miss Morland my stupid sister has mistaken all your clearest expressions. You talked of expected horrors in London and instead of instantly conceiving, as any rational creature would have done, that such words could relate only to a circulating library, she immediately pictured to herself a mob of three thousand men assembling in St. George's Fields, the Bank attacked, the Tower threatened, the streets of London flowing with blood, a detachment of the Twelfth Light Dragoons (the hopes of the nation) called up from Northampton to quell the insurgents, and the gallant Captain Frederick Tilney, in the moment of charging at the head of his troop, knocked off his horse by a brickbat from an upper window. Forgive her stupidity. The fears of the sister have added to the weakness of the woman; but she is by no means a simpleton in general.'

Catherine looked grave. 'And now, Henry,' said Miss Tilney, 'that you have made us understand each other, you may as well make Miss Morland understand yourself unless you mean to have her think you intolerably rude to your sister, and a great brute in your opinion of women in general. Miss Morland is not used to your odd ways.'

Note: Henry Tilney enjoys novels as much as Catherine and several contemporary authors are mentioned. The riot mentioned occurred in 1780.

CHAPTER 17

The entrance of her father put a stop to the civility, which Catherine was beginning to hope might introduce a desire of their corresponding. After addressing her with his usual politeness, he turned to his daughter and said, 'Well, Eleanor, may I congratulate you on being successful in your application to your fair friend?'

'I was just beginning to make the request, sir, as you came in.'

'Well, proceed by all means. I know how much your heart is in it. My daughter, Miss Morland,' he continued, without leaving his daughter time to speak, 'has been forming a very bold wish. We leave Bath, as she has perhaps told you, on Saturday se'nnight. A letter from my steward tells me that my presence is wanted at home; and being disappointed in my hope of seeing the Marquis of Longtown and General Courteney here, some of my very old friends, there is nothing to detain me longer in Bath. And could we carry our selfish point with you, we should leave it without a single regret. Can you, in short, be prevailed on to quit this scene of public triumph and oblige your friend Eleanor with your company in Gloucestershire? I am almost ashamed to make the request, though its presumption would certainly appear greater to every creature in Bath than yourself. Modesty such as yours but not for the world would I pain it by open praise. If you can be induced to honour us with a visit, you will make us happy beyond expression. 'Tis true, we can offer you nothing like the gaieties of this lively place; we can tempt you neither by amusement nor splendour, for our mode of living, as you see, is plain and unpretending; yet no endeavours shall be wanting on our side to make Northanger Abbey not wholly disagreeable.'

Northanger Abbey! These were thrilling words, and wound up Catherine's feelings to the highest point of ecstasy. Her grateful and gratified heart could hardly restrain its expressions within the language of tolerable calmness. To receive so flattering an invitation! To have her company so warmly solicited! Everything honourable and soothing, every present enjoyment, and every future hope was contained in it; and her acceptance, with only the saving clause of Papa and Mamma's approbation, was eagerly given.

General Tilney was not less sanguine, having already waited on her excellent friends in Pulteney Street, and obtained their sanction of his wishes. 'Since they can consent to part with you,' said he, 'we may expect philosophy from all the world.'

Miss Tilney was earnest, though gentle, in her secondary civilities, and the affair became in a few minutes as nearly settled as this necessary reference to Fullerton would allow.

The circumstances of the morning had led Catherine's feelings through the varieties of suspense, security, and disappointment; but they were now safely lodged in perfect bliss; and with spirits elated to rapture, with Henry at her heart, and Northanger Abbey on her lips, she hurried home to write her letter. Mr. and Mrs. Morland, relying on the discretion of the friends to whom they had already entrusted their daughter, felt no doubt of the propriety of an acquaintance which had been formed under their eye, and sent therefore by return of post their ready consent to her visit in Gloucestershire. This indulgence, though not more than Catherine had hoped for, completed her conviction of being favoured beyond every other human creature, in friends and fortune, circumstance and chance. Everything seemed to cooperate for her advantage. By the kindness of her first friends, the Allens, she had been introduced into scenes where pleasures of every kind had met her. Her feelings, her preferences, had each known the happiness of a return. Wherever she felt attachment, she had been able to create it. The affection of Isabella was to be secured to her in a sister. The Tilneys, they, by whom, above all, she desired to be favourably thought of, outstripped even her wishes in the flattering measures by which their intimacy was to be continued. She was to be their chosen visitor, she was to be for weeks under the same roof with the person whose society she mostly prized and, in addition to all the rest, this roof was to be the roof of an abbey! Her passion for ancient edifices was next in degree to her passion for Henry Tilney and castles and abbeys made usually the charm of those reveries which his image did not fill. To see and explore either the ramparts and keep of the one, or the cloisters of the other, had been for many weeks a darling wish, though to be more than the visitor of an hour had seemed too nearly impossible for desire. And yet, this was to happen. With all the chances against her of house, hall, place, park, court, and cottage, Northanger turned up an abbey, and she was to be its inhabitant. Its long, damp passages, its narrow cells and ruined chapel, were to be within her daily reach, and she could not entirely subdue the hope of some traditional legends, some awful memorials of an injured and ill-fated nun.

It was wonderful that her friends should seem so little elated by the possession of such a home, that the consciousness of it should be so meekly borne. The power of early habit only could account for it. A distinction to which they had been born gave no pride. Their superiority of abode was no more to them than their superiority of person.

Many were the inquiries she was eager to make of Miss Tilney; but so active were her thoughts, that when these inquiries were answered, she was hardly more assured than before, of Northanger Abbey having been a richly endowed convent at the time of the Reformation, of its having fallen into the hands of an ancestor of the Tilneys on its dissolution, of a large portion of the ancient building still making a part of the present dwelling although the rest was decayed, or of its standing low in a valley, sheltered from the north and east by rising woods of oak.

Note: the word 'Abbey' suggests it is an ancient and distinguished building. Between 1535-1540 the monasteries in England were bought or given away.

CHAPTER 20

At last, however, the door was closed upon the three females, and they set off at the sober pace in which the handsome, highly fed four horses of a gentleman usually perform a journey of thirty miles: such was the distance of Northanger from Bath, to be now divided into two equal stages.

The remembrance of Mr. Allen's opinion, respecting young men's open carriages, made her blush at the mention of such a plan, and her first thought was to decline it; but her second was of greater deference for General Tilney's judgment; he could not propose anything improper for her;

and, in the course of a few minutes, she found herself with Henry in the curricle, as happy a being as ever existed.

He smiled, and said, 'You have formed a very favourable idea of the abbey.'

'To be sure, I have. Is not it a fine old place, just like what one reads about?'

'And are you prepared to encounter all the horrors that a building such as 'what one reads about' may produce? Have you a stout heart? Nerves fit for sliding panels and tapestry?'

'Oh! yes I do not think I should be easily frightened, because there would be so many people in the house and besides, it has never been uninhabited and left deserted for years, and then the family come back to it unawares, without giving any notice, as generally happens.'

'No, certainly. We shall not have to explore our way into a hall dimly lighted by the expiring embers of a wood fire nor be obliged to spread our beds on the floor of a room without windows, doors, or furniture. But you must be aware that when a young lady is (by whatever means) introduced into a dwelling of this kind, she is always lodged apart from the rest of the family. While they snugly repair to their own end of the house, she is formally conducted by Dorothy, the ancient housekeeper, up a different staircase, and along many gloomy passages, into an apartment never used since some cousin or kin died in it about twenty years before. Can you stand such a ceremony as this? Will not your mind misgive you when you find yourself in this gloomy chamber too lofty and extensive for you, with only the feeble rays of a single lamp to take in its size its walls hung with tapestry exhibiting figures as large as life, and the bed, of dark green stuff or purple velvet, presenting even a funereal appearance? Will not your heart sink within you?'

'Oh! But this will not happen to me, I am sure.'

'How fearfully will you examine the furniture of your apartment! And what will you discern? Not tables, toilettes, wardrobes, or drawers, but on one side perhaps the remains of a broken lute, on the other a ponderous chest which no efforts can open, and over the fireplace the portrait of some handsome warrior, whose features will so incomprehensibly strike you, that you will not be able to withdraw your eyes from it. Dorothy, meanwhile, no less struck by your appearance, gazes on you in great agitation, and drops a few unintelligible hints. To raise your spirits, moreover, she gives you reason to suppose that the part of the abbey you inhabit is undoubtedly haunted, and informs you that you will not have a single domestic within call. With this parting cordial she curtsies off you listen to the sound of her receding footsteps as long as the last echo can reach you and when, with fainting spirits, you attempt to fasten your door, you discover, with increased alarm, that it has no lock.'

'Oh! Mr. Tilney, how frightful! This is just like a book! But it cannot really happen to me. I am sure your housekeeper is not really Dorothy. Well, what then?'

'Nothing further to alarm perhaps may occur the first night. After surmounting your unconquerable horror of the bed, you will retire to rest, and get a few hours' unquiet slumber. But on the second, or at farthest the third night after your arrival, you will probably have a violent storm. Peals of thunder so loud as to seem to shake the edifice to its foundation will roll round the neighbouring mountains and during the frightful gusts of wind which accompany it, you will probably think you discern (for your lamp is not extinguished) one part of the hanging more violently agitated than the rest. Unable of course to repress your curiosity in so favourable a moment for indulging it, you will instantly arise, and throwing your dressing-gown around you, proceed to examine this mystery. After a very short search, you will discover a division in the tapestry so artfully constructed as to defy the minutest inspection, and on opening it, a door will immediately appear which door, being only secured by massy bars and a padlock, you will, after a few efforts, succeed in opening and, with your lamp in your hand, will pass through it into a small vaulted room.'

'No, indeed; I should be too much frightened to do any such thing.'

'What! Not when Dorothy has given you to understand that there is a secret subterraneous communication between your apartment and the chapel of St. Anthony, scarcely two miles off? Could you shrink from so simple an adventure? No, no, you will proceed into this small vaulted room, and through this into several others, without perceiving anything very remarkable in either. In one perhaps there may be a dagger, in another a few drops of blood, and in a third the remains of some instrument of torture; but there being nothing in all this out of the common way, and your lamp being nearly exhausted, you will return towards your own apartment. In repassing through the small vaulted room, however, your eyes will be attracted towards a large, old-fashioned cabinet of ebony and gold, which, though narrowly examining the furniture before, you had passed unnoticed. Impelled by an irresistible presentiment, you will eagerly advance to it, unlock its folding doors, and search into every drawer but for some time without discovering anything of importance perhaps nothing but a considerable hoard of diamonds. At last, however, by touching a secret spring, an inner compartment will open a roll of paper appears you seize it it contains many sheets of manuscript you hasten with the precious treasure into your own chamber, but scarcely have you been able to decipher 'Oh! Thou whomsoever thou mayst be, into whose hands these memoirs of the wretched Matilda may fall' when your lamp suddenly expires in the socket, and leaves you in total darkness.'

'Oh! No, no do not say so. Well, go on.'

But Henry was too much amused by the interest he had raised to be able to carry it farther; he could no longer command solemnity either of subject or voice, and was obliged to entreat her to use her own fancy in the perusal of Matilda's woes. Catherine, recollecting herself, grew ashamed of her eagerness, and began earnestly to assure him that her attention had been fixed without the smallest apprehension of really meeting with what he related. 'Miss Tilney, she was sure, would never put her into such a chamber as he had described! She was not at all afraid.'

As they drew near the end of their journey, her impatience for a sight of the abbey for some time suspended by his conversation on subjects very different returned in full force, and every bend in the road was expected with solemn awe to afford a glimpse of its massy walls of grey stone, rising amidst a grove of ancient oaks, with the last beams of the sun playing in beautiful splendour on its high Gothic windows. But so low did the building stand, that she found herself passing through the great gates of the lodge into the very grounds of Northanger, without having discerned even an antique chimney.

She knew not that she had any right to be surprised, but there was a something in this mode of approach which she certainly had not expected. To pass between lodges of a modern appearance, to find herself with such ease in the very precincts of the abbey, and driven so rapidly along a smooth, level road of fine gravel, without obstacle, alarm, or solemnity of any kind, struck her as odd and inconsistent. She was not long at leisure, however, for such considerations. A sudden scud of rain, driving full in her face, made it impossible for her to observe anything further, and fixed all her thoughts on the welfare of her new straw bonnet; and she was actually under the abbey walls, was springing, with Henry's assistance, from the carriage, was beneath the shelter of the old porch, and had even passed on to the hall, where her friend and the general were waiting to welcome her, without feeling one awful foreboding of future misery to herself, or one moment's suspicion of any past scenes of horror being acted within the solemn edifice. The breeze had not seemed to waft the sighs of the murdered to her; it had wafted nothing worse than a thick mizzling rain; and having given a good shake to her habit, she was ready to be shown into the common drawing-room, and capable of considering where she was.

An abbey! Yes, it was delightful to be really in an abbey! But she doubted, as she looked round the room, whether anything within her observation would have given her the consciousness. The furniture was in all the profusion and elegance of modern taste. The fireplace, where she had expected the ample width and ponderous carving of former times, was contracted to a Rumford, with slabs of plain though handsome marble, and ornaments over it of the prettiest English china. The windows, to which she looked with peculiar dependence, from having heard the general talk of his preserving them in their Gothic form with reverential care, were yet less what her fancy had portrayed. To be sure, the pointed arch was preserved the form of them was Gothic they might be even casements but every pane was so large, so clear, so light! To an imagination which had hoped for the smallest divisions, and the heaviest stone-work, for painted glass, dirt, and cobwebs, the difference was very distressing.

The general, perceiving how her eye was employed, began to talk of the smallness of the room and simplicity of the furniture, where everything, being for daily use, pretended only to comfort, etc.; flattering himself, however, that there were some apartments in the Abbey not unworthy her notice and was proceeding to mention the costly gilding of one in particular, when, taking out his watch, he stopped short to pronounce it with surprise within twenty minutes of five! This seemed the word of separation, and Catherine found herself hurried away by Miss Tilney in such a manner as convinced her that the strictest punctuality to the family hours would be expected at Northanger.

Returning through the large and lofty hall, they ascended a broad staircase of shining oak, which, after many flights and many landing-places, brought them upon a long, wide gallery. On one side it had a range of doors, and it was lighted on the other by windows which Catherine had only time to discover looked into a quadrangle, before Miss Tilney led the way into a chamber, and scarcely staying to hope she would find it comfortable, left her with an anxious entreaty that she would make as little alteration as possible in her dress.

Note: when Catherine reaches the Abbey she is disappointed to find it modern, comfortable and well lit. The pointed arch is typical of the gothic style.

CHAPTER 21

A moment's glance was enough to satisfy Catherine that her apartment was very unlike the one which Henry had endeavoured to alarm her by the description of. It was by no means unreasonably large, and contained neither tapestry nor velvet. The walls were papered, the floor was carpeted; the windows were neither less perfect nor more dim than those of the drawing-room below; the furniture, though not of the latest fashion, was handsome and comfortable, and the air of the room altogether far from uncheerful. Her heart instantaneously at ease on this point, she resolved to lose no time in particular examination of anything, as she greatly dreaded disobliging the general by any delay. Her habit therefore was thrown off with all possible haste, and she was preparing to unpin the linen package, which the chaise-seat had conveyed for her immediate accommodation, when her eye suddenly fell on a large high chest, standing back in a deep recess on one side of the fireplace. The sight of it made her start; and, forgetting everything else, she stood gazing on it in motionless wonder, while these thoughts crossed her:

'This is strange indeed! I did not expect such a sight as this! An immense heavy chest! What can it hold? Why should it be placed here? Pushed back too, as if meant to be out of sight! I will look into it cost me what it may, I will look into it and directly too by daylight. If I stay till evening my candle may go out.' She advanced and examined it closely: it was of cedar, curiously inlaid with some darker wood, and raised, about a foot from the ground, on a carved stand of the same. The lock was silver, though tarnished from age; at each end were the imperfect remains of handles also of silver, broken perhaps prematurely by some strange violence; and, on the centre of the lid, was a mysterious cipher, in the same metal. Catherine bent over it intently, but without being able to distinguish anything with certainty. She could not, in whatever direction she took it, believe the last letter to be a T; and yet that it should be anything else in that house was a circumstance to raise no common degree of astonishment. If not originally theirs, by what strange events could it have fallen into the Tilney family?

Her fearful curiosity was every moment growing greater; and seizing, with trembling hands, the hasp of the lock, she resolved at all hazards to satisfy herself at least as to its contents. With difficulty, for something seemed to resist her efforts, she raised the lid a few inches; but at that moment a sudden knocking at the door of the room made her, starting, quit her hold, and the lid closed with alarming violence. This ill-timed intruder was Miss Tilney's maid, sent by her mistress to be of use to Miss Morland; and though Catherine immediately dismissed her, it recalled her to the sense of what she ought to be doing, and forced her, in spite of her anxious desire to penetrate this mystery, to proceed in her dressing without further delay. Her progress was not quick, for her thoughts and her eyes were still bent on the object so well calculated to interest and alarm; and though she dared not waste a moment upon a second attempt, she could not remain many paces from the chest. At length, however, having slipped one arm into her gown, her toilette seemed so nearly finished that the impatience of her curiosity might safely be indulged. One moment surely might be spared; and, so desperate should be the exertion of her strength, that, unless secured by supernatural means, the lid in one moment should be thrown back. With this spirit she sprang forward, and her confidence did not deceive her. Her resolute effort threw back the lid, and gave to her astonished eyes the view of a white cotton counterpane, properly folded, reposing at one end of the chest in undisputed possession!

She was gazing on it with the first blush of surprise when Miss Tilney, anxious for her friend's being ready, entered the room, and to the rising shame of having harboured for some minutes an absurd expectation, was then added the shame of being caught in so idle a search. 'That is a curious old chest, is not it?' said Miss Tilney, as Catherine hastily closed it and turned away to the glass. 'It is impossible to say how many generations it has been here. How it came to be first put in this room I know not, but I have not had it moved, because I thought it might sometimes be of use in holding hats and bonnets. The worst of it is that its weight makes it difficult to open. In that corner, however, it is at least out of the way.'

Catherine had no leisure for speech, being at once blushing, tying her gown, and forming wise resolutions with the most violent dispatch. Miss Tilney gently hinted her fear of being late; and in half a minute they ran downstairs together, in an alarm not wholly unfounded, for General Tilney was pacing the drawing-room, his watch in his hand, and having, on the very instant of their entering, pulled the bell with violence, ordered 'Dinner to be on table directly!'

Catherine trembled at the emphasis with which he spoke, and sat pale and breathless, in a most humble mood, concerned for his children, and detesting old chests; and the general, recovering his politeness as he looked at her, spent the rest of his time in scolding his daughter for so foolishly hurrying her fair friend, who was absolutely out of breath from haste, when there was not the least occasion for hurry in the world: but Catherine could not at all get over the double distress of having involved her friend in a lecture and been a great simpleton herself, till they were happily seated at the dinner-table, when the general's complacent smiles, and a good appetite of her own, restored her to peace. The dining-parlour was a noble room, suitable in its dimensions to a much larger drawing-room than the one in common use, and fitted up in a style of luxury and expense which was almost lost on the unpractised eye of Catherine, who saw little more than its spaciousness and the number of their attendants. Of the former, she spoke aloud her admiration; and the general, with a very gracious countenance, acknowledged that it was by no means an ill-sized room, and further confessed that, though as careless on such subjects as most people, he did look upon a tolerably large eating-room as one of the necessaries of life; he supposed, however, 'that she must have been used to much better-sized apartments at Mr. Allen's?'

'No, indeed,' was Catherine's honest assurance; 'Mr. Allen's dining-parlour was not more than half as large,' and she had never seen so large a room as this in her life. The general's good humour increased. Why, as he had such rooms, he thought it would be simple not to make use of them; but, upon his honour, he believed there might be more comfort in rooms of only half their size. Mr. Allen's house, he was sure, must be exactly of the true size for rational happiness.

The evening passed without any further disturbance, and, in the occasional absence of General Tilney, with much positive cheerfulness. It was only in his presence that Catherine felt the smallest fatigue from her journey; and even then, even in moments of languor or restraint, a sense of general happiness preponderated, and she could think of her friends in Bath without one wish of being with them.

The night was stormy; the wind had been rising at intervals the whole afternoon; and by the time the party broke up, it blew and rained violently. Catherine, as she crossed the hall, listened to the tempest with sensations of awe; and, when she heard it rage round a corner of the ancient building and close with sudden fury a distant door, felt for the first time that she was really in an abbey. Yes, these were characteristic sounds; they brought to her recollection a countless variety of dreadful situations and horrid scenes, which such buildings had witnessed, and such storms ushered in; and most heartily did she rejoice in the happier circumstances attending her entrance within walls so solemn! She had nothing to dread from midnight assassins or drunken gallants. Henry had certainly been only in jest in what he had told her that morning. In a house so furnished, and so guarded, she could have nothing to explore or to suffer, and might go to her bedroom as securely as if it had been her own chamber at Fullerton. Thus wisely fortifying her mind, as she proceeded upstairs, she was enabled, especially on perceiving that Miss Tilney slept only two doors from her, to enter her room with a tolerably stout heart; and her spirits were immediately assisted by the cheerful blaze of a wood fire. 'How much better is this,' said she, as she walked to the fender 'how much better to find a fire ready lit, than to have to wait shivering in the cold till all the family are in bed, as so many poor girls have been obliged to do, and then to have a faithful old servant frightening one by coming in with a faggot! How glad I am that Northanger is what it is! If it had been like some other places, I do not know that, in such a night as this, I could have answered for my courage: but now, to be sure, there is nothing to alarm one.'

She looked round the room. The window curtains seemed in motion. It could be nothing but the violence of the wind penetrating through the divisions of the shutters; and she stepped boldly forward, carelessly humming a tune, to assure herself of its being so, peeped courageously behind each curtain, saw nothing on either low window seat to scare her, and on placing a hand against the shutter, felt the strongest conviction of the wind's force. A glance at the old chest, as she turned away from this examination, was not without its use; she scorned the causeless fears of an idle fancy, and began with a most happy indifference to prepare herself for bed. 'She should take her time; she should not hurry herself; she did not care if she were the last person up in the house. But she would not make up her fire; that would seem cowardly, as if she wished for the protection of light after she were in bed.' The fire therefore died away, and Catherine, having spent the best part of an hour in her arrangements, was beginning to think of stepping into bed, when, on giving a parting glance round the room, she was struck by the appearance of a high, old-fashioned black cabinet, which, though in a situation conspicuous enough, had never caught her notice before. Henry's words, his description of the ebony cabinet which was to escape her observation at first, immediately rushed across her; and though there could be nothing really in it, there was something whimsical, it was certainly a very remarkable coincidence! She took her candle and looked closely at the cabinet. It was not absolutely ebony and gold; but it was japan, black and yellow japan of the handsomest kind; and as she held her candle, the yellow had very much the effect of gold. The key was in the door, and she had a strange fancy to look into it; not, however, with the smallest expectation of finding anything, but it was so very odd, after what Henry had said. In short, she could not sleep till she had examined it. So, placing the candle with great caution on a chair, she seized the key with a very tremulous hand and tried to turn it; but it resisted her utmost strength. Alarmed, but not discouraged, she tried it another way; a bolt flew, and she believed herself successful; but how strangely mysterious! The door was still immovable. She paused a moment in breathless wonder. The wind roared down the chimney, the rain beat in torrents against the windows, and everything seemed to speak the awfulness of her situation. To retire to bed, however, unsatisfied on such a point, would be vain, since sleep must be impossible with the consciousness of a cabinet so mysteriously closed in her immediate vicinity. Again, therefore, she applied herself to the key, and after moving it in every possible way for some instants with the determined celerity of hope's last effort, the door suddenly yielded to her hand: her heart leaped with exultation at such a victory, and having thrown open each folding door, the second being secured only by bolts of less wonderful construction than the lock, though in that her eye could not discern anything unusual, a double range of small drawers appeared in view, with some larger drawers above and below them; and in the centre, a small door, closed also with a lock and key, secured in all probability a cavity of importance.

Catherine's heart beat quick, but her courage did not fail her. With a cheek flushed by hope, and an eye straining with curiosity, her fingers grasped the handle of a drawer and drew it forth. It was entirely empty. With less alarm and greater eagerness she seized a second, a third, a fourth; each was equally empty. Not one was left unsearched, and in not one was anything found. Well read in the art of concealing a treasure, the possibility of false linings to the drawers did not escape her, and she felt round each with anxious acuteness in vain. The place in the middle alone remained now unexplored; and though she had 'never from the first had the smallest idea of finding anything in any part of the cabinet, and was not in the least disappointed at her ill success thus far, it would be foolish not to examine it thoroughly while she was about it.' It was some time however before she could unfasten the door, the same difficulty occurring in the management of this inner lock as of the outer; but at length it did open; and not vain, as hitherto, was her search; her quick eyes directly fell on a roll of paper pushed back into the further part of the cavity, apparently for concealment, and her feelings at that moment were indescribable. Her heart fluttered, her knees trembled, and her cheeks grew pale. She seized, with an unsteady hand, the precious manuscript, for half a glance sufficed to ascertain written characters; and while she acknowledged with awful sensations this striking exemplification of what Henry had foretold, resolved instantly to peruse every line before she attempted to rest.

The dimness of the light her candle emitted made her turn to it with alarm; but there was no danger of its sudden extinction; it had yet some hours to burn; and that she might not have any greater difficulty in distinguishing the writing than what its ancient date might occasion, she hastily snuffed it. Alas! It was snuffed and extinguished in one. A lamp could not have expired with more awful effect. Catherine, for a few moments, was motionless with horror. It was done completely; not a remnant of light in the wick could give hope to the rekindling breath. Darkness impenetrable and immovable filled the room. A violent gust of wind, rising with sudden fury, added fresh horror to the moment. Catherine trembled from head to foot. In the pause which succeeded, a sound like receding footsteps and the closing of a distant door struck on her affrighted ear. Human nature could support no more. A cold sweat stood on her forehead, the manuscript fell from her hand, and groping her way to the bed, she jumped hastily in, and sought some suspension of agony by creeping far underneath the clothes. To close her eyes in sleep that night, she felt must be entirely out of the question. With a curiosity so justly awakened, and feelings in every way so agitated, repose must be absolutely impossible. The storm too abroad so dreadful! She had not been used to feel alarm from wind, but now every blast seemed fraught with awful intelligence. The manuscript so wonderfully found, so wonderfully accomplishing the morning's prediction, how was it to be accounted for? What could it contain? To whom could it relate? By what means could it have been so long concealed?

And how singularly strange that it should fall to her lot to discover it! Till she had made herself mistress of its contents, however, she could have neither repose nor comfort; and with the sun's first rays she was determined to peruse it. But many were the tedious hours which must yet intervene. She shuddered, tossed about in her bed, and envied every quiet sleeper. The storm still raged, and various were the noises, more terrific even than the wind, which struck at intervals on her startled ear. The very curtains of her bed seemed at one moment in motion, and at another the lock of her door was agitated, as if by the attempt of somebody to enter. Hollow murmurs seemed to creep along the gallery, and more than once her blood was chilled by the sound of distant moans. Hour after hour passed away, and the wearied Catherine had heard three proclaimed by all the clocks in the house before the tempest subsided or she unknowingly fell fast asleep.

Note: to 'snuff a candle' is either to remove part of the wick with a special instrument in order to keep it alight, or the extinguish it. In the chapter above it means the former.

CHAPTER 22

The housemaid's folding back her window-shutters at eight o'clock the next day was the sound which first roused Catherine; and she opened her eyes, wondering that they could ever have been closed, on objects of cheerfulness; her fire was already burning, and a bright morning had succeeded the tempest of the night. Instantaneously, with the consciousness of existence, returned her recollection of the manuscript; and springing from the bed in the very moment of the maid's going away, she eagerly collected every scattered sheet which had burst from the roll on its falling to the ground, and flew back to enjoy the luxury of their perusal on her pillow. She now plainly saw that she must not expect a manuscript of equal length with the generality of what she had shuddered over in books, for the roll, seeming to consist entirely of small disjointed sheets, was altogether but of trifling size, and much less than she had supposed it to be at first.

Her greedy eye glanced rapidly over a page. She started at its import. Could it be possible, or did not her senses play her false? An inventory of linen, in coarse and modern characters, seemed all that was before her! If the evidence of sight might be trusted, she held a washing-bill in her hand. She seized another sheet, and saw the same articles with little variation; a third, a fourth, and a fifth presented nothing new. Shirts, stockings, cravats, and waistcoats faced her in each. Two others, penned by the same hand, marked an expenditure scarcely more interesting, in letters, hair-powder, shoe-string, and breeches-ball. And the larger sheet, which had enclosed the rest, seemed by its first cramp line, 'To poultice chestnut mare' a farrier's bill! Such was the collection of papers (left perhaps, as she could then suppose, by the negligence of a servant in the place whence she had taken them) which had filled her with expectation and alarm, and robbed her of half her night's rest! She felt humbled to the dust. Could not the adventure of the chest have taught her wisdom? A corner of it, catching her eye as she lay, seemed to rise up in judgment against her. Nothing could now be clearer than the absurdity of her recent fancies. To suppose that a manuscript of many generations back could have remained undiscovered in a room such as that, so modern, so habitable! Or that she should be the first to possess the skill of unlocking a cabinet, the key of which was open to all!

How could she have so imposed on herself? Heaven forbid that Henry Tilney should ever know her folly! And it was in a great measure his own doing, for had not the cabinet appeared so exactly to agree with his description of her adventures, she should never have felt the smallest curiosity about it. This was the only comfort that occurred. Impatient to get rid of those hateful evidences of her folly, those detestable papers then scattered over the bed, she rose directly, and folding them up as nearly as possible in the same shape as before, returned them to the same spot within the cabinet, with a very hearty wish that no untoward accident might ever bring them forward again, to disgrace her even with herself.

Why the locks should have been so difficult to open, however, was still something remarkable, for she could now manage them with perfect ease. In this there was surely something mysterious, and she indulged in the flattering suggestion for half a minute, till the possibility of the door's having been at first unlocked, and of being herself its fastener, darted into her head, and cost her another blush.

She got away as soon as she could from a room in which her conduct produced such unpleasant reflections, and found her way with all speed to the breakfast-parlour, as it had been pointed out to her by Miss Tilney the evening before. Henry was alone in it; and his immediate hope of her having been undisturbed by the tempest, with an arch reference to the character of the building they inhabited, was rather distressing. For the world would she not have her weakness suspected, and yet, unequal to an absolute falsehood, was constrained to acknowledge that the wind had kept her awake a little.

Catherine did not exactly know how this was to be understood. Why was Miss Tilney embarrassed? Could there be any unwillingness on the general's side to show her over the abbey? The proposal was his own. And was not it odd that he should always take his walk so early? Neither her father nor Mr. Allen did so. It was certainly very provoking. She was all impatience to see the house, and had scarcely any curiosity about the grounds. If Henry had been with them indeed! But now she should not know what was picturesque when she saw it. Such were her thoughts, but she kept them to herself, and put on her bonnet in patient discontent.

She was struck, however, beyond her expectation, by the grandeur of the abbey, as she saw it for the first time from the lawn. The whole building enclosed a large court; and two sides of the quadrangle, rich in Gothic ornaments, stood forward for admiration. The remainder was shut off by knolls of old trees, or luxuriant plantations, and the steep woody hills rising behind, to give it shelter, were beautiful even in the leafless month of March. Catherine had seen nothing to compare with it; and her feelings of delight were so strong, that without waiting for any better authority, she boldly burst forth in wonder and praise. The general listened with assenting gratitude; and it seemed as if his own estimation of Northanger had waited unfixed till that hour.

Note: an inventory of linen is a laundry bill. Catherine suspects some family mystery due to the sadness with which Eleanor speaks of her dead mother.

CHAPTER 23

She ventured, when next alone with Eleanor, to express her wish of being permitted to see it, as well as all the rest of that side of the house; and Eleanor promised to attend her there, whenever they should have a convenient hour. Catherine understood her: the general must be watched from home, before that room could be entered. 'It remains as it was, I suppose?' said she, in a tone of feeling.

'Yes, entirely.'

'And how long ago may it be that your mother died?'

'She has been dead these nine years.' And nine years, Catherine knew, was a trifle of time, compared with what generally elapsed after the death of an injured wife, before her room was put to rights.

'You were with her, I suppose, to the last?'

'No,' said Miss Tilney, sighing; 'I was unfortunately from home. Her illness was sudden and short; and, before I arrived it was all over.'

Catherine's blood ran cold with the horrid suggestions which naturally sprang from these words. Could it be possible? Could Henry's father ? And yet how many were the examples to justify even the blackest suspicions! And, when she saw him in the evening, while she worked with her friend, slowly pacing the drawing-room for an hour together in silent thoughtfulness, with downcast eyes and contracted brow, she felt secure from all possibility of wronging him. It was the air and attitude of a Montoni! What could more plainly speak the gloomy workings of a mind not wholly dead to every sense of humanity, in its fearful review of past scenes of guilt? Unhappy man! And the anxiousness of her spirits directed her eyes towards his figure so repeatedly, as to catch Miss Tilney's notice. 'My father,' she whispered, 'often walks about the room in this way; it is nothing unusual.'

'So much the worse!' thought Catherine; such ill-timed exercise was of a piece with the strange unseasonableness of his morning walks, and boded nothing good.

To be kept up for hours, after the family were in bed, by stupid pamphlets was not very likely. There must be some deeper cause: something was to be done which could be done only while the household slept; and the probability that Mrs. Tilney yet lived, shut up for causes unknown, and receiving from the pitiless hands of her husband a nightly supply of coarse food, was the conclusion which necessarily followed. Shocking as was the idea, it was at least better than a death unfairly hastened, as, in the natural course of things, she must ere long be released. The suddenness of her reputed illness, the absence of her daughter, and probably of her other children, at the time all favoured the supposition of her imprisonment. Its origin jealousy perhaps, or wanton cruelty was yet to be unravelled.

In revolving these matters, while she undressed, it suddenly struck her as not unlikely that she might that morning have passed near the very spot of this unfortunate woman's confinement might have been within a few paces of the cell in which she languished out her days; for what part of the abbey could be more fitted for the purpose than that which yet bore the traces of monastic division? In the high-arched passage, paved with stone, which already she had trodden with peculiar awe, she well remembered the doors of which the general had given no account. To what might not those doors lead? In support of the plausibility of this conjecture, it further occurred to her that the forbidden gallery, in which lay the apartments of the unfortunate Mrs. Tilney, must be, as certainly as her memory could guide her, exactly over this suspected range of cells, and the staircase by the side of those apartments of which she had caught a transient glimpse, communicating by some secret means with those cells, might well have favoured the barbarous proceedings of her husband. Down that staircase she had perhaps been conveyed in a state of well-prepared insensibility!

Catherine sometimes started at the boldness of her own surmises, and sometimes hoped or feared that she had gone too far; but they were supported by such appearances as made their dismissal impossible.

The side of the quadrangle, in which she supposed the guilty scene to be acting, being, according to her belief, just opposite her own, it struck her that, if judiciously watched, some rays of light from the general's lamp might glimmer through the lower windows, as he passed to the prison of his wife; and, twice before she stepped into bed, she stole gently from her room to the corresponding window in the gallery, to see if it appeared; but all abroad was dark, and it must yet be too early. The various ascending noises convinced her that the servants must still be up. Till midnight, she supposed it would be in vain to watch; but then, when the clock had struck twelve, and all was quiet, she would, if not quite appalled by darkness, steal out and look once more. The clock struck twelve and Catherine had been half an hour asleep.

Note: Catherine's reference to 'stupid pamphlets' indicates she has very little time for history or politics.

CHAPTER 24

In the course of this morning's reflections, she came to a resolution of making her next attempt on the forbidden door alone. It would be much better in every respect that Eleanor should know nothing of the matter. To involve her in the danger of a second detection, to court her into an apartment which must wring her heart, could not be the office of a friend. The general's utmost anger could not be to herself what it might be to a daughter; and, besides, she thought the examination itself would be more satisfactory if made without any companion. It would be impossible to explain to Eleanor the suspicions, from which the other had, in all likelihood, been hitherto happily exempt; nor could she therefore, in her presence, search for those proofs of the general's cruelty, which however they might yet have escaped discovery, she felt confident of somewhere drawing forth, in the shape of some fragmented journal, continued to the last gasp. Of the way to the apartment she was now perfectly mistress; and as she wished to get it over before Henry's return, who was expected on the morrow, there was no time to be lost. The day was bright, her courage high; at four o'clock, the sun was now two hours above the horizon, and it would be only her retiring to dress half an hour earlier than usual.

It was done; and Catherine found herself alone in the gallery before the clocks had ceased to strike. It was no time for thought; she hurried on, slipped with the least possible noise through the folding doors, and without stopping to look or breathe, rushed forward to the one in question. The lock yielded to her hand, and, luckily, with no sullen sound that could alarm a human being. On tiptoe she entered; the room was before her; but it was some minutes before she could advance another step. She beheld what fixed her to the spot and agitated every feature. She saw a large, well-proportioned apartment, an handsome dimity bed, arranged as unoccupied with an housemaid's care, a bright Bath stove, mahogany wardrobes, and neatly painted chairs, on which the warm beams of a western sun gaily poured through two sash windows! Catherine had expected to have her feelings worked, and worked they were. Astonishment and doubt first seized them; and a shortly succeeding ray of common sense added some bitter emotions of shame. She could not be mistaken as to the room; but how grossly mistaken in everything else! in Miss Tilney's meaning, in her own calculation! This apartment, to which she had given a date so ancient, a position so awful, proved to be one end of what the general's father had built. There were two other doors in the chamber, leading probably into dressing-closets; but she had no inclination to open either. Would the veil in which Mrs. Tilney had last walked, or the volume in which she had last read, remain to tell what nothing else was allowed to whisper? No: whatever might have been the general's crimes, he had certainly too much wit to let them sue for detection. She was sick of exploring, and desired but to be safe in her own room, with her own heart only privy to its folly; and she was on the point of retreating as softly as she had entered, when the sound of footsteps, she could hardly tell where, made her pause and tremble. To be found there, even by a servant, would be unpleasant; but by the general (and he seemed always at hand when least wanted), much worse! She listened the sound had ceased; and resolving not to lose a moment, she passed through and closed the door. At that instant a door underneath was hastily opened; someone seemed with swift steps to ascend the stairs, by the head of which she had yet to pass before she could gain the gallery. She had no power to move. With a feeling of terror not very definable, she fixed her eyes on the staircase, and in a few moments it gave Henry to her view. 'Mr. Tilney!' she exclaimed in a voice of more than common astonishment. He looked astonished too. 'Good God!' she continued, not attending to his address. 'How came you here? How came you up that staircase?'

'How came I up that staircase!' he replied, greatly surprised. 'Because it is my nearest way from the stable-yard to my own chamber; and why should I not come up it?'

Catherine recollected herself, blushed deeply, and could say no more. He seemed to be looking in her countenance for that explanation which her lips did not afford. She moved on towards the gallery. 'And may I not, in my turn,' said he, as he pushed back the folding doors, 'ask how you came here? This passage is at least as extraordinary a road from the breakfast-parlour to your apartment, as that staircase can be from the stables to mine.'

'I have been,' said Catherine, looking down, 'to see your mother's room.'

'My mother's room! Is there anything extraordinary to be seen there?'

'No, nothing at all. I thought you did not mean to come back till tomorrow.'

'I did not expect to be able to return sooner, when I went away; but three hours ago I had the pleasure of finding nothing to detain me. You look pale. I am afraid I alarmed you by running so fast up those stairs. Perhaps you did not know you were not aware of their leading from the offices in common use?'

'No, I was not. You have had a very fine day for your ride.'

'Very; and does Eleanor leave you to find your way into all the rooms in the house by yourself?'

'Oh! No; she showed me over the greatest part on Saturday and we were coming here to these rooms but only' dropping her voice 'your father was with us.'

'And that prevented you,' said Henry, earnestly regarding her. 'Have you looked into all the rooms in that passage?'

'No, I only wanted to see Is not it very late? I must go and dress.'

'It is only a quarter past four' showing his watch 'and you are not now in Bath. No theatre, no rooms to prepare for. Half an hour at Northanger must be enough.'

She could not contradict it, and therefore suffered herself to be detained, though her dread of further questions made her, for the first time in their acquaintance, wish to leave him. They walked slowly up the gallery. 'Have you had any letter from Bath since I saw you?'

'No, and I am very much surprised. Isabella promised so faithfully to write directly.'

'Promised so faithfully! A faithful promise! That puzzles me. I have heard of a faithful performance. But a faithful promise the fidelity of promising! It is a power little worth knowing, however, since it can deceive and pain you.

My mother's room is very commodious, is it not? Large and cheerful-looking, and the dressing-closets so well disposed! It always strikes me as the most comfortable apartment in the house, and I rather wonder that Eleanor should not take it for her own. She sent you to look at it, I suppose?'

'No.'

'It has been your own doing entirely?' Catherine said nothing. After a short silence, during which he had closely observed her, he added, 'As there is nothing in the room in itself to raise curiosity, this must have proceeded from a sentiment of respect for my mother's character, as described by Eleanor, which does honour to her memory. The world, I believe, never saw a better woman. But it is not often that virtue can boast an interest such as this. The domestic, unpretending merits of a person never known do not often create that kind of fervent, venerating tenderness which would prompt a visit like yours. Eleanor, I suppose, has talked of her a great deal?'

'Yes, a great deal. That is no, not much, but what she did say was very interesting. Her dying so suddenly' (slowly, and with hesitation it was spoken), 'and you none of you being at home and your father, I thought perhaps had not been very fond of her.'

'And from these circumstances,' he replied (his quick eye fixed on hers), 'you infer perhaps the probability of some negligence some' (involuntarily she shook her head) 'or it may be of something still less pardonable.' She raised her eyes towards him more fully than she had ever done before. 'My mother's illness,' he continued, 'the seizure which ended in her death, was sudden. The malady itself, one from which she had often suffered, a bilious fever its cause therefore constitutional. On the third day, in short, as soon as she could be prevailed on, a physician attended her, a very respectable man, and one in whom she had always placed great confidence. Upon his opinion of her danger, two others were called in the next day, and remained in almost constant attendance for four and twenty hours. On the fifth day she died. During the progress of her disorder, Frederick and I (we were both at home) saw her repeatedly; and from our own observation can bear witness to her having received every possible attention which could spring from the affection of those about her, or which her situation in life could command. Poor Eleanor was absent, and at such a distance as to return only to see her mother in her coffin.'

'But your father,' said Catherine, 'was he afflicted?'

'For a time, greatly so. You have erred in supposing him not attached to her. He loved her, I am persuaded, as well as it was possible for him to we have not all, you know, the same tenderness of disposition and I will not pretend to say that while she lived, she might not often have had much to bear, but though his temper injured her, his judgment never did. His value of her was sincere; and, if not permanently, he was truly afflicted by her death.'

'I am very glad of it,' said Catherine; 'it would have been very shocking!'

'If I understand you rightly, you had formed a surmise of such horror as I have hardly words to Dear Miss Morland, consider the dreadful nature of the suspicions you have entertained. What have you been judging from? Remember the country and the age in which we live. Remember that we are English, that we are Christians. Consult your own understanding, your own sense of the probable, your own observation of what is passing around you. Does our education prepare us for such atrocities? Do our laws connive at them? Could they be perpetrated without being known, in a country like this, where social and literary intercourse is on such a footing, where every man is surrounded by a neighbourhood of voluntary spies, and where roads and newspapers lay everything open? Dearest Miss Morland, what ideas have you been admitting?'

They had reached the end of the gallery, and with tears of shame she ran off to her own room.

Note: Catherine is surprised by Henry's unexpected return from his parsonage and foolishly shares her wild surmises.

CHAPTER 25

The visions of romance were over. Catherine was completely awakened. Henry's address, short as it had been, had more thoroughly opened her eyes to the extravagance of her late fancies than all their several disappointments had done. Most grievously was she humbled. Most bitterly did she cry. It was not only with herself that she was sunk but with Henry. Her folly, which now seemed even criminal, was all exposed to him, and he must despise her forever. The liberty which her imagination had dared to take with the character of his father could he ever forgive it? The absurdity of her curiosity and her fears could they ever be forgotten? She hated herself more than she could express. He had she thought he had, once or twice before this fatal morning, shown something like affection for her. But now in short, she made herself as miserable as possible for about half an hour, went down when the clock struck five, with a broken heart, and could scarcely give an intelligible answer to Eleanor's inquiry if she was well. The formidable Henry soon followed her into the room, and the only difference in his behaviour to her was that he paid her rather more attention than usual. Catherine had never wanted comfort more, and he looked as if he was aware of it.

The evening wore away with no abatement of this soothing politeness; and her spirits were gradually raised to a modest tranquillity. She did not learn either to forget or defend the past; but she learned to hope that it would never transpire farther, and that it might not cost her Henry's entire regard. Her thoughts being still chiefly fixed on what she had with such causeless terror felt and done, nothing could shortly be clearer than that it had been all a voluntary, self-created delusion, each trifling circumstance receiving importance from an imagination resolved on alarm, and everything forced to bend to one purpose by a mind which, before she entered the abbey, had been craving to be frightened. She remembered with what feelings she had prepared for a knowledge of Northanger. She saw that the infatuation had been created, the mischief settled, long before her quitting Bath, and it seemed as if the whole might be traced to the influence of that sort of reading which she had there indulged.

Charming as were all Mrs. Radcliffe's works, and charming even as were the works of all her imitators, it was not in them perhaps that human nature, at least in the Midland counties of England, was to be looked for. Of the Alps and Pyrenees, with their pine forests and their vices, they might give a faithful delineation; and Italy, Switzerland, and the south of France might be as fruitful in horrors as they were there represented. Catherine dared not doubt beyond her own country, and even of that, if hard pressed, would have yielded the northern and western extremities. But in the central part of England there was surely some security for the existence even of a wife not beloved, in the laws of the land, and the manners of the age. Murder was not tolerated, servants were not slaves, and neither poison nor sleeping potions to be procured, like rhubarb, from every druggist. Among the Alps and Pyrenees, perhaps, there were no mixed characters. There, such as were not as spotless as an angel might have the dispositions of a fiend. But in England it was not so; among the English, she believed, in their hearts and habits, there was a general though unequal mixture of good and bad. Upon this conviction, she would not be surprised if even in Henry and Eleanor Tilney, some slight imperfection might hereafter appear; and upon this conviction she need not fear to acknowledge some actual specks in the character of their father, who, though cleared from the grossly injurious suspicions which she must ever blush to have entertained, she did believe, upon serious consideration, to be not perfectly amiable.

Her mind made up on these several points, and her resolution formed, of always judging and acting in future with the greatest good sense, she had nothing to do but to forgive herself and be happier than ever; and the lenient hand of time did much for her by insensible gradations in the course of another day. Henry's astonishing generosity and nobleness of conduct, in never alluding in the slightest way to what had passed, was of the greatest assistance to her; and sooner than she could have supposed it possible in the beginning of her distress, her spirits became absolutely comfortable, and capable, as heretofore, of continual improvement by anything he said.

Note: Catherine has, for the most part, realised the error of her ways; appreciating that gothic literature cannot teach her anything about 'civilised' England.

CHAPTER 30

She was guilty only of being less rich than he [General Tilney] had supposed her to be. Under a mistaken persuasion of her possessions and claims, he had courted her acquaintance in Bath, solicited her company at Northanger, and designed her for his daughter-in-law. On discovering his error, to turn her from the house seemed the best, though to his feelings an inadequate proof of his resentment towards herself, and his contempt of her family.

John Thorpe had first misled him. The general, perceiving his son one night at the theatre to be paying considerable attention to Miss Morland, had accidentally inquired of Thorpe if he knew more of her than her name. Thorpe, most happy to be on speaking terms with a man of General Tilney's importance, had been joyfully and proudly communicative; and being at that time not only in daily expectation of Morland's engaging Isabella, but likewise pretty well resolved upon marrying Catherine himself, his vanity induced him to represent the family as yet more wealthy than his vanity and avarice had made him believe them. With whomsoever he was, or was likely to be connected, his own consequence always required that theirs should be great, and as his intimacy with any acquaintance grew, so regularly grew their fortune. The expectations of his friend Morland, therefore, from the first overrated, had ever since his introduction to Isabella been gradually increasing; and by merely adding twice as much for the grandeur of the moment, by doubling what he chose to think the amount of Mr.

Morland's preferment, trebling his private fortune, bestowing a rich aunt, and sinking half the children, he was able to represent the whole family to the general in a most respectable light. For Catherine, however, the peculiar object of the general's curiosity, and his own speculations, he had yet something more in reserve, and the ten or fifteen thousand pounds which her father could give her would be a pretty addition to Mr. Allen's estate. Her intimacy there had made him seriously determine on her being handsomely legacied hereafter; and to speak of her therefore as the almost acknowledged future heiress of Fullerton naturally followed. Upon such intelligence the general had proceeded; for never had it occurred to him to doubt its authority. Thorpe's interest in the family, by his sister's approaching connection with one of its members, and his own views on another (circumstances of which he boasted with almost equal openness), seemed sufficient vouchers for his truth; and to these were added the absolute facts of the Allens being wealthy and childless, of Miss Morland's being under their care, and as soon as his acquaintance allowed him to judge of their treating her with parental kindness. His resolution was soon formed. Already had he discerned a liking towards Miss Morland in the countenance of his son; and thankful for Mr. Thorpe's communication, he almost instantly determined to spare no pains in weakening his boasted interest and ruining his dearest hopes. Catherine herself could not be more ignorant at the time of all this, than his own children. Henry and Eleanor, perceiving nothing in her situation likely to engage their father's particular respect, had seen with astonishment the suddenness, continuance, and extent of his attention; and though latterly, from some hints which had accompanied an almost positive command to his son of doing everything in his power to attach her, Henry was convinced of his father's believing it to be an advantageous connection, it was not till the late explanation at Northanger that they had the smallest idea of the false calculations which had hurried him on. That they were false, the general had learnt from the very person who had suggested them, from Thorpe himself, whom he had chanced to meet again in town, and who, under the influence of exactly opposite feelings, irritated by Catherine's refusal, and yet more by the failure of a very recent endeavour to accomplish a reconciliation between Morland and Isabella, convinced that they were separated forever, and spurning a friendship which could be no longer serviceable, hastened to contradict all that he had said before to the advantage of the Morlands confessed himself to have been totally mistaken in his opinion of their circumstances and character, misled by the rhodomontade of his friend to believe his father a man of substance and credit, whereas the transactions of the two or three last weeks proved him to be neither; for after coming eagerly forward on the first overture of a marriage between the families, with the most liberal proposals, he had, on being brought to the point by the shrewdness of the relator, been constrained to acknowledge himself incapable of giving the young people even a decent support. They were, in fact, a necessitous family; numerous, too, almost beyond example; by no means respected in their own neighbourhood, as he had lately had particular opportunities of discovering; aiming at a style of life which their fortune could not warrant; seeking to better themselves by wealthy connections; a forward, bragging, scheming race.

The terrified general pronounced the name of Allen with an inquiring look; and here too Thorpe had learnt his error. The Allens, he believed, had lived near them too long, and he knew the young man on whom the Fullerton estate must devolve. The general needed no more. Enraged with almost everybody in the world but himself, he set out the next day for the abbey, where his performances have been seen.

I leave it to my reader's sagacity to determine how much of all this it was possible for Henry to communicate at this time to Catherine, how much of it he could have learnt from his father, in what points his own conjectures might assist him, and what portion must yet remain to be told in a letter from James. I have united for their case what they must divide for mine. Catherine, at any rate, heard enough to feel that in suspecting General Tilney of either murdering or shutting up his wife, she had scarcely sinned against his character, or magnified his cruelty.

Henry, in having such things to relate of his father, was almost as pitiable as in their first avowal to himself. He blushed for the narrow-minded counsel which he was obliged to expose. The conversation between them at Northanger had been of the most unfriendly kind. Henry's indignation on hearing how Catherine had been treated, on comprehending his father's views, and being ordered to acquiesce in them, had been open and bold. The general, accustomed on every ordinary occasion to give the law in his family, prepared for no reluctance but of feeling, no opposing desire that should dare to clothe itself in words, could ill brook the opposition of his son, steady as the sanction of reason and the dictate of conscience could make it. But, in such a cause, his anger, though it must shock, could not intimidate Henry, who was sustained in his purpose by a conviction of its justice. He felt himself bound as much in honour as in affection to Miss Morland, and believing that heart to be his own which he had been directed to gain, no unworthy retraction of a tacit consent, no reversing decree of unjustifiable anger, could shake his fidelity, or influence the resolutions it prompted.

He steadily refused to accompany his father into Herefordshire, an engagement formed almost at the moment to promote the dismissal of Catherine, and as steadily declared his intention of offering her his hand. The general was furious in his anger, and they parted in dreadful disagreement. Henry, in an agitation of mind which many solitary hours were required to compose, had returned almost instantly to Woodston, and, on the afternoon of the following day, had begun his journey to Fullerton.

Note: the word rhodomontade means vain and empty boasting. It is worth noting the repeated use of the first person pronoun 'I' and the compressed feel to the penultimate chapter.

CHAPTER 31

Mr. and Mrs. Morland's surprise on being applied to by Mr. Tilney for their consent to his marrying their daughter was, for a few minutes, considerable, it having never entered their heads to suspect an attachment on either side; but as nothing, after all, could be more natural than Catherine's being beloved, they soon learnt to consider it with only the happy agitation of gratified pride, and, as far as they alone were concerned, had not a single objection to start. His pleasing manners and good sense were self-evident recommendations; and having never heard evil of him, it was not their way to suppose any evil could be told. Goodwill supplying the place of experience, his character needed no attestation. 'Catherine would make a sad, heedless young housekeeper to be sure,' was her mother's foreboding remark; but quick was the consolation of there being nothing like practice.

There was but one obstacle, in short, to be mentioned; but till that one was removed, it must be impossible for them to sanction the engagement. Their tempers were mild, but their principles were steady, and while his parent so expressly forbade the connection, they could not allow themselves to encourage it. That the general should come forward to solicit the alliance, or that he should even very heartily approve it, they were not refined enough to make any parading stipulation; but the decent appearance of consent must be yielded, and that once obtained and their own hearts made them trust that it could not be very long denied their willing approbation was instantly to follow. His consent was all that they wished for. They were no more inclined than entitled to demand his money. Of a very considerable fortune, his son was, by marriage settlements, eventually secure; his present income was an income of independence and comfort, and under every pecuniary view, it was a match beyond the claims of their daughter.

The young people could not be surprised at a decision like this. They felt and they deplored but they could not resent it; and they parted, endeavouring to hope that such a change in the general, as each believed almost impossible, might speedily take place, to unite them again in the fullness of privileged affection. Henry returned to what was now his only home, to watch over his young plantations, and extend his improvements for her sake, to whose share in them he looked anxiously forward; and Catherine remained at Fullerton to cry. Whether the torments of absence were softened by a clandestine correspondence, let us not inquire. Mr. and Mrs. Morland never did they had been too kind to exact any promise; and whenever Catherine received a letter, as, at that time, happened pretty often, they always looked another way.

The anxiety, which in this state of their attachment must be the portion of Henry and Catherine, and of all who loved either, as to its final event, can hardly extend, I fear, to the bosom of my readers, who will see in the tell-tale compression of the pages before them, that we are all hastening together to perfect felicity. The means by which their early marriage was effected can be the only doubt: what probable circumstance could work upon a temper like the general's? The circumstance which chiefly availed was the marriage of his daughter with a man of fortune and consequence, which took place in the course of the summer an accession of dignity that threw him into a fit of good humour, from which he did not recover till after Eleanor had obtained his forgiveness of Henry, and his permission for him 'to be a fool if he liked it!'

The marriage of Eleanor Tilney, her removal from all the evils of such a home as Northanger had been made by Henry's banishment, to the home of her choice and the man of her choice, is an event which I expect to give general satisfaction among all her acquaintance. My own joy on the occasion is very sincere. I know no one more entitled, by unpretending merit, or better prepared by habitual suffering, to receive and enjoy felicity. Her partiality for this gentleman was not of recent origin; and he had been long withheld only by inferiority of situation from addressing her. His unexpected accession to title and fortune had removed all his difficulties; and never had the general loved his daughter so well in all her hours of companionship, utility, and patient endurance as when he first hailed her 'Your Ladyship!' Her husband was really deserving of her; independent of his peerage, his wealth, and his attachment, being to a precision the most charming young man in the world. Any further definition of his merits must be unnecessary; the most charming young man in the world is instantly before the imagination of us all. Concerning the one in question, therefore, I have only to add aware that the rules of composition forbid the introduction of a character not connected with my fable that this was the very gentleman whose negligent servant left behind him that collection of washing-bills, resulting from a long visit at Northanger, by which my heroine was involved in one of her most alarming adventures.

The influence of the viscount and viscountess in their brother's behalf was assisted by that right understanding of Mr. Morland's circumstances which, as soon as the general would allow himself to be informed, they were qualified to give. It taught him that he had been scarcely more misled by Thorpe's first boast of the family wealth than by his subsequent malicious overthrow of it; that in no sense of the word were they necessitous or poor, and that Catherine would have three thousand pounds. This was so material an amendment of his late expectations that it greatly contributed to smooth the descent of his pride; and by no means without its effect was the private intelligence, which he was at some pains to procure, that the Fullerton estate, being entirely at the disposal of its present proprietor, was consequently open to every greedy speculation.

On the strength of this, the general, soon after Eleanor's marriage, permitted his son to return to Northanger, and thence made him the bearer of his consent, very courteously worded in a page full of empty professions to Mr. Morland. The event which it authorized soon followed: Henry and Catherine were married, the bells rang, and everybody smiled; and, as this took place within a twelvemonth from the first day of their meeting, it will not appear, after all the dreadful delays occasioned by the general's cruelty, that they were essentially hurt by it. To begin perfect happiness at the respective ages of twenty-six and eighteen is to do pretty well; and professing myself moreover convinced that the general's unjust interference, so far from being really injurious to their felicity, was perhaps rather conducive to it, by improving their knowledge of each other, and adding strength to their attachment, I leave it to be settled, by whomsoever it may concern, whether the tendency of this work be altogether to recommend parental tyranny, or reward filial disobedience.

Note: approval for the marriage is given. Again, there is the repeated use of 'I' and the denouement is rapidly given.

A NOTE ON THE TEXT

Northanger Abbey was written in 1797-98 under a different title. The manuscript was revised around 1803 and sold to a London publisher, Crosbie & Co., who sold it back in 1816. This text is based on the first edition, published by John Murray, London, in 1818 the year following Miss Austen's death. Spelling and punctuation have been largely brought into conformity with modern British usage.

Jane Austen – A Short Biography

Our understanding of the author, beyond the pages of her novels, is limited with biographical information being infamously scarce. For example, relatively few of her personal letters remain (approximately160 out of the 3,000 or so letters estimated to have been written by the author) and academics have unearthed little information over the last century, with most of the biographical material produced after Austen's death having been written by her relatives and reflecting the 'good quiet Aunt Jane'.

However, we do know that Jane Austen was born on the16th December 1775 in a small village called Steventon in Hampshire. She lived her entire life as part of a close-knit family located on the lower fringes of the English landed gentry. She was educated primarily by her father and older brothers as well as through her own reading. The steadfast support of her family was critical to her development as a professional writer. From her teenage years into her thirties she experimented with various literary forms, including an epistolary novel which she then abandoned, wrote and extensively revised three major novels and began a fourth. From 1811 until 1816, with the release of *Sense and Sensibility* (1811), *Pride and Prejudice* (1813), *Mansfield Park* (1814) and *Emma* (1815), she achieved success as a published writer. She wrote two additional novels, *Northanger Abbey* and *Persuasion*, though both were published posthumously in 1818. She had begun a third, which was eventually titled *Sanditon*, but died in Winchester of a wasting disease before completing it on the 18th July, 1817.

Austen's works critique the novels of sensibility of the second half of the 18th century and are part of the transition to 19th-century realism. Her plots, though fundamentally comic, highlight the dependence of women on marriage to secure social standing and economic security. Her works, though usually popular, were first published anonymously and brought her little personal fame and only a few positive reviews during her lifetime, but the publication in 1869 of her nephew's *A*

Memoir of Jane Austen introduced her to a wider public, and by the 1940s she had become widely accepted in academia as a great English writer.

Jane Austen – A Natural Historian

Jane Austen has often been praised as a natural historian. She is a naturalist among tame animals. She does not study man (as Dostoevsky does) in his wild state before he has been domesticated. Her men and women are essentially men and women of the fireside.

Nor is Jane Austen entirely a realist in her treatment even of these. She idealizes them to the point of making most of them good-looking, and she hates poverty to such a degree that she seldom can endure to write about anybody who is poor. She is not happy in the company of a character who has not at least a thousand pounds. 'People get so horridly poor and economical in this part of the world,' she writes on one occasion, 'that I have no patience with them. Kent is the only place for happiness; everybody is rich there.' Her novels do not introduce us to the most exalted levels of the aristocracy. They provide us, however, with a natural history of county people and of people who are just below the level of county people and live in the eager hope of being taken notice of by them. There is more caste snobbishness, I think, in Jane Austen's novels than in any other fiction of equal genius. She, far more than Thackeray, is the novelist of snobs.

How far Jane Austen herself shared the social prejudices of her characters it is not easy to say. Unquestionably, she satirized them. At the same time, she imputes the sense of superior rank not only to her butts, but to her heroes and heroines, as no other novelist has ever done. Emma Woodhouse lamented the deficiency of this sense in Frank Churchill. 'His indifference to a confusion of rank,' she thought, 'bordered too much on inelegance of mind.' Mr. Darcy, again, even when he melts so far as to become an avowed lover, neither forgets his social position, nor omits to talk about it. 'His sense of her inferiority, of its being a degradation ... was dwelt on with a warmth which seemed due to the consequence he was wounding, but was very unlikely to recommend his suit.' On discovering, to his amazement, that Elizabeth is offended rather than overwhelmed by his condescension, he defends himself warmly. 'Disguise of every sort,' he declares, 'is my abhorrence. Nor am I ashamed of the feelings I related. They were natural and just. Could you expect me to rejoice in the inferiority of your connections? To congratulate myself on the hope of relations whose condition in life is so decidedly beneath my own?'

It is perfectly true that Darcy and Emma Woodhouse are the butts of Miss Austen as well as being among her heroes and heroines. She mocks them - Darcy especially - no less than she admires. She loves to let her wit play about the egoism of social caste. She is quite merciless in deriding, it when it becomes overbearing, as in Lady Catherine de Bourgh, or when it produces flunkeyish reactions, as in Mr. Collins. But I fancy she liked a modest measure of it. Most people do. Jane Austen, in writing so much about the sense of family and position, chose as her theme one of the most widespread passions of civilized human nature.

She was herself a clergyman's daughter. She was the seventh of a family of eight, born in the parsonage at Steventon, in Hampshire. Her life seems to have been far from exciting. Her father, like the clergy in her novels, was a man of leisure; of so much leisure, as Mr. Cornish reminds us, that he was able to read out Cowper to his family in the mornings. Jane was brought up to be a young lady of leisure. She learned French and Italian and sewing: she was 'especially great in satin-stitch.' She excelled at the game of spillikins.

She must have begun to write at an early age. In later life, she urges an ambitious niece, aged twelve, to give up writing till she is sixteen, adding that 'she had herself often wished she had read more and written less in the corresponding years of her life.' She was only twenty when she began to write First Impressions, the perfect book which was not published till seventeen years later with the title altered to Pride and Prejudice. She wrote secretly for many years. Her family knew of it, but the world did not, not even the servants or the visitors to the house. She used to hide the little sheets of paper on which she was writing when any one approached. She had not, apparently, a room to herself, and must have written under constant threat of interruption. She objected to having a creaking door mended on one occasion, because she knew by it when any one was coming.

She got little encouragement to write. *Pride and Prejudice* was offered to a publisher in 1797: he would not even read it. *Northanger Abbey* was written in the next two years. It was not accepted by a publisher, however, till 1803; and he, having paid ten pounds for it, refused to publish it. One of Miss Austen's brothers bought back the manuscript at the price at which it had been sold twelve or thirteen years later; but even then it was not published till 1818, when the author was dead.

The first of her books to appear was *Sense and Sensibility*. She had begun to write it immediately after finishing *Pride and Prejudice*. It was published in 1811, a good many years later, when Miss Austen was thirty-six years old. The title-page merely said that it was written 'By a Lady.' The author never put her name to any of her books. For an anonymous first novel, it must be admitted, *Sense and Sensibility* was not unsuccessful. It brought Miss Austen £150; 'a prodigious recompense,' she thought, 'for that which had cost her nothing.' The fact, however, that she had not earned more than £700 from her novels by the time of her death shows that she never became a really popular author in her lifetime.

She was rewarded as poorly in credit as in cash, though the Prince Regent became an enthusiastic admirer of her books, and kept a set of them in each of his residences. It was the Prince Regent's librarian, the Rev. J.S. Clarke, who, on becoming chaplain to Prince Leopold of Saxe-Coburg, made the suggestion to her that 'an historical romance, illustrative of the history of the august House of Coburg, would just now be very interesting.' Mr. Collins, had he been able to wean himself from Fordyce's Sermons so far as to allow himself to take an interest in fiction, could hardly have made a proposal more exquisitely grotesque. One is glad the proposal was made, however, not only for its own sake, but because it drew an admirable reply from Miss Austen on the nature of her genius. 'I could not sit seriously down,' she declared, 'to write a serious romance under any other motive than to save my life; and, if it were indispensable for me to keep it up, and never relax into laughing at myself or at other people, I am sure I should be hung before I had finished the first chapter.'

Jane Austen knew herself for what she was, an inveterate laugher. She belonged essentially to the eighteenth century, the century of the wits. She enjoyed the spectacle of men and women making fools of themselves, and she did not hide her enjoyment under a pretence of unobservant good-nature. She observed with malice. It is tolerably certain that Miss Mitford was wrong in accepting the description of her in private life as 'perpendicular, precise, taciturn, a poker of whom everyone is afraid.' Miss Austen, one is sure, was a lady of good-humour, as well as a novelist of good-humour; but the good-humour had a flavour. It was the good-humour of the satirist, not of the sentimentalizer. One can imagine Jane Austen herself speaking as Elizabeth Bennet once spoke to her monotonously soft-worded sister. 'That is the most unforgiving speech,' she said, 'that I ever heard you utter. Good girl!'

Miss Austen has even been accused of irreverence, and we occasionally find her in her letters as irreverent in the presence of death as Mr. Shaw. 'Only think,' she writes in one letter - a remark she works into a chapter of *Emma* - 'of Mrs. Holder being dead! Poor woman, she has done the only thing in the world she could possibly do to make one cease to abuse her.' And on another occasion she writes: 'Mrs. Hall, of Sherborne, was brought to bed yesterday of a dead child, some weeks before she expected, owing to a fright. I suppose she happened unawares to look at her husband.' It is possible that Miss Austen's sense of the comic ran away with her at times as Emma Woodhouse's did. I do not know of any similar instance of cruelty in conversation on the part of a likeable person so unpardonable as Emma Woodhouse's witticism at the expense of Miss Bates at the Box Hill picnic. Miss Austen makes Emma ashamed of her witticism, however, after Mr. Knightley has lectured her for it. She sets a limit to the rights of wit, again, in *Pride and Prejudice*, when Elizabeth defends her sharp tongue against Darcy. 'The wisest and best of men,' ... he protests, 'may be rendered ridiculous by a person whose first object in life is a joke.' 'I hope I never ridicule what is wise or good,' says Elizabeth in the course of her answer. 'Follies and nonsense, whims and inconsistencies, do divert me, I own, and I laugh at them whenever I can.' The six novels that Jane Austen has left us might be described as the record of the diversions of a clergyman's daughter.

The diversions of Jane Austen were, beyond those of most novelists, the diversions of a spectator. (That is what Scott and Macaulay meant by comparing her to Shakespeare.) Or, rather, they were the diversions of a listener. She observed with her ears rather than with her eyes. With her, conversation was three-fourths of life. Her stories are stories of people who reveal themselves almost exclusively in talk. She wastes no time in telling us what people and places looked like. She will dismiss a man or a house or a view or a dinner with an adjective such as 'handsome.' There is more description of persons and places in Mr. Shaw's stage-directions than in all Miss Austen's novels. She cuts the 'osses and comes to the cackle as no other English novelist of the same eminence has ever done. If we know anything of the setting or character or even the appearance of her men and women, it is due far more to what they say than to anything that is said about them. And yet how perfect is her gallery of portraits! One can guess the very angle of Mr. Collins's toes.

One seems, too, to be able to follow her characters through the trivial round of the day's idleness as closely as if one were pursuing them under the guidance of a modern realist. They are the most unoccupied people, I think, who ever lived in literature. They are people in whose lives a slight fall of snow is an event. Louisa Musgrave's jump on the Cobb at Lyme Regis produces more commotion in the Jane Austen world than murder and arson do in an ordinary novel. Her people do not even seem, for the most part, to be interested in anything but their opinions of each other. They have few passions beyond match-making. They are unconcerned about any of the great events of their time. Almost the only reference in the novels to the Napoleonic Wars is a mention of the prize-money of naval officers. 'Many a noble fortune,' says Mr. Shepherd in *Persuasion*, 'has been made during the war.' Miss Austen's principal use of the Navy outside Mansfield Park is as a means of portraying the exquisite vanity of Sir Walter Elliott - his inimitable manner of emphasizing the importance of both rank and good looks in the make-up of a gentleman. 'The profession has its utility,' he says of the Navy, 'but I should be sorry to see any friend of mine belonging to it.' He goes on to explain his reasons: 'It is in two points offensive to me; I have two strong grounds of objection to it. First as being the means of bringing persons of obscure birth into undue distinction, and raising men to honour which their fathers and grandfathers never dreamt of; and, secondly, as it cuts up a man's youth and vigour most terribly; a sailor grows older sooner than any other man.'

Sir Walter complains that he had once had to give place at dinner to Lord St. Ives, the son of a curate, and 'a certain Admiral Baldwin, the most deplorable-looking personage you can imagine: his face the colour of mahogany, rough and rugged to the last degree, all lines and wrinkles, nine grey hairs of a side, and nothing but a dab of powder at top':

'In the name of heaven, who is that old fellow?' said I to a friend of mine who was standing near (Sir Basil Morley). 'Old fellow!' cried Sir Basil, 'it is Admiral Baldwin. What do you take his age to be?' 'Sixty,' said I, 'or perhaps sixty-two.' 'Forty,' replied Sir Basil, 'forty, and no more.' Picture to yourselves my amazement; I shall not easily forget Admiral Baldwin. I never saw quite so wretched an example of what a sea-faring life can do; but to a degree, I know, it is the same with them all; they are all knocked about, and exposed to every climate and every weather, till they are not fit to be seen. It is a pity they are not knocked on the head at once, before they reach Admiral Baldwin's age.

That, I think, is an excellent example of Miss Austen's genius for making her characters talk. Luckily, conversation was still formal in her day, and it was as possible for her as for Congreve to make middling men and women talk first-rate prose. She did more than this, however. She was the first English novelist before Meredith to portray charming women with free personalities. Elizabeth Bennet and Emma Woodhouse have an independence (rare in English fiction) of the accident of being fallen in love with. Elizabeth is a delightful prose counterpart of Beatrice.

Miss Austen has another point of resemblance to Meredith besides that which I have mentioned. She loves to portray men puffed up with self-approval. She, too, is a satirist of the male egoist. Her books are the most finished social satires in English fiction. They are so perfect in the delicacy of their raillery as to be charming. One is conscious in them, indeed, of the presence of a sparkling spirit. Miss Austen comes as near being a star as it is possible to come in eighteenth-century conversational prose. She used to say that, if ever she should marry, she would fancy being Mrs. Crabbe. She had much of Crabbe's realism, indeed; but what a dance she led realism with the mocking light of her wit!

Robert Lynd

13521143R00070

Printed in Great Britain
by Amazon.co.uk, Ltd.,
Marston Gate.